THE TWISTED TRAIL

THE TWISTED TRAIL

•

L. W. Rogers

CARO AREA DISTRICT LIBRARY
840 W. FRANK STREET
CARO, MICHIGAN 48723

AVALON BOOKS
NEW YORK

© Copyright 2008 by Loretta Rogers
All rights reserved.
All the characters in this book are fictitious,
and any resemblance to actual persons,
living or dead, is purely coincidental.
Published by Thomas Bouregy & Co., Inc.
160 Madison Avenue, New York, NY 10016

Library of Congress Cataloging-in-Publication Data
Rogers, L.W.
The Twisted trail / L.W. Rogers.
    p. cm.
ISBN 978-0-8034-9891-4 (acid-free paper)
I. Title.
PS36183.O46469T86   2008
813'.6—dc22   2007037211

PRINTED IN THE UNITED STATES OF AMERICA
ON ACID-FREE PAPER
BY HADDON CRAFTSMEN, BLOOMSBURG, PENNSYLVANIA

To my husband, Wayne, for wearing headphones so the television wouldn't disturb me while writing and for his understanding about a writer's deadlines.

Special thanks to my critique partner, Wilma Fasano, and to my readers, with much affection and deepest appreciation.

Preface

Steeped in the rich history of cowboys, cattle raising, red-light districts, and Seminole and Miccosukee Indians, Florida is now and always has been more of a cattle state than most states west of the Mississippi.

Although fiction this Cracker Western is rooted in fact and details that are historically correct. In the 1840s, what was then known as Fort Brooke is now Tampa, Florida.

Long before the 1849 California Gold Rush, "Thar's gold in them thar hills" echoed through Georgia's Dahlonega foothills and Nacoochee-Helen Valley. For over a century, hoards of miners extracted thousands of pounds of gold from these foothills.

It was the discovery of gold which led to the push

that eventually removed the Cherokee and Creek Indians from their homelands in Georgia.

I would like to express my gratitude to the historians, whose dedication has preserved that era, allowing the rest of us to cherish its spirit of freedom.

Chapter One

Like vultures, the three gunmen waited for the stagecoach carrying the man they'd been hired to kill. They sat in the sun on their horses among the rocks on the jagged crest of the hill, and gazed north along the route down which the stagecoach would travel on its way to Fort Brooke.

The road snaked emptily toward them through a sun-scorched, barren land of eroded foothills and wind-rippled sand dunes. Except for an occasional dust devil there was nothing moving between the waiting killers and the horizon.

Sun gleamed on the far-distant hills. Although well into fall, the men had ridden hard all morning, and this far south the sun still burned strong enough to take its toll of men and horses.

"No telling how long it'll be 'til that stage shows up,"

4 *L. W. Rogers*

grumbled Bowles, a heavy, harsh-faced man in his late twenties. "Might have to wait here the rest of the day."

"So we'll wait," Driscoll told him flatly. Driscoll's stocky figure slouched in the saddle while he surveyed the distances, his arrogant, mocking brown eyes squinted against the blazing sun. Two days' growth of beard showed a soft red-gold fuzz.

The youngest of the three men, Driscoll enjoyed using his guns, and his quick temper afforded him the unquestionable position as leader of the trio.

Bowles scratched his bristly black stubble and tugged his hat forward to shade his eyes more. "Henry Denham better be aboard like he's supposed to be. Elsewise we've wasted a lot of riding for nothing."

"Denham's due in Fort Brooke by tonight," Driscoll pointed out. "And there's just the one stage through today."

"Mebbe he won't come by stage. Could be he decided to ride south on his own, like we did."

"Could be," Driscoll acknowledged carelessly. "But why would he? Denham ain't expecting trouble."

He removed his hat, revealing a tangled thatch of red hair, and wiped a hand across his wide forehead. Shaking drops of sweat from his thick stubby fingers, he glanced at the third man, Munoz, a lean old-timer with a seamed leathery face.

"No sense us all baking our brains out," he told Munoz with easy authority. "You settle here and keep watch. We'll mosey down to the stage station. If the

The Twisted Trail 5

stage don't show in a couple of hours, I'll send Bowles to relieve you."

Munoz, some twenty-five years older than Driscoll, accepted his order without question. He merely nodded, climbed off his horse, and found himself a patch of shade between two boulders from which he had a clear view of the road. Driscoll turned his mount and headed south toward the small stage station huddled out of sight at the foot of the hills.

Bowles followed and caught up with him. For a few moments he rode in silence beside Driscoll. Then he spoke up carefully, out of deference to the younger man's judgment. "I sure hope you're right about Denham bein' on the stage. If he gets to Fort Brooke, we don't get paid."

Driscoll grinned boyishly. "He'll get to Fort Brooke, all right. Only not alive."

Matthew Logan reached the stage station on foot, carrying his saddle gear across his shoulder and a twelve-shot Winchester .44 carbine in his left hand. Dust caked thick on his clothes and formed a mask on his lean, strong-boned face. The sun had baked him dry and his long legs were heavy with fatigue. His boots hadn't been designed for hours of hiking across rough country.

He paused next to a tangle of rocks and dog fennels, his widespread blue eyes taking in the buildings by the road—a sable palm log shack and a small barn. He noted six horses in the rope corral, grouped close in

6   *L. W. Rogers*

the patch of dark shade thrown by the barn wall. With a sigh of relief, Logan strode on toward the open-doored shack.

Inside, Driscoll, Bowles, and the station manager sat around the table playing poker. Driscoll sat where he could watch through the open door and single window. He was the first to notice the approach of the tall, wide-shouldered, lanky man. He noted the stranger's battered work Stetson, old buckskin shirt, and well-worn Levis, and pegged him for a cowhand.

"Company coming," he announced.

The plump, middle-aged station manager turned in his chair and looked. "What d'you know. Walkin'—" He placed his cards facedown, shoved to his feet, and went out to meet the newcomer.

"Looks like you've had trouble," he greeted Logan amiably.

"My horse broke a leg yesterday afternoon. Any chance of buying one of yours?"

The station manager shook his head. "'Ceptin' for the stage remounts only got one, and he ain't for sale."

Logan glanced toward the corral.

"Them other two ain't mine," the station manager explained. "Belong to a coupla fellers just taking a rest inside before riding on. But there's a stage coming through today. Going on south to Fort Brooke. Whereabouts you headed?"

"Fort Brooke will do. When's the stage expected?"

"Now. Which might mean three hours from now."

When Logan smiled it softened the set of his wide

The Twisted Trail

mouth and crinkles appeared through the dust at the corners of his eyes. "Time enough. I could use a wash. So could my clothes. Been a long walk."

"Cost you a dollar."

The price was reasonable. A man could expect a free drink, but water for anything else came dear in Florida's drought season. He nodded. "I've got a dollar."

From inside the shack, Driscoll and Bowles watched Logan follow the chubby man into the barn.

"Reckon he'll be a problem," Bowles said.

The young redhead shrugged. "Any extra gun's an extra problem. I reckon he'll be easy enough to take care of."

Before the station manager returned from the barn, Driscoll explained his plan to Bowles.

Left alone in the barn with a cut-down barrel half filled with water, Logan dropped his hat and gunbelt next to the carbine and saddlebags, and pulled off his boots. Before shrugging out of his shirt, he glanced toward the doorway to make sure no one lurked about to watch him. A narrow-bladed knife in a soft buckskin sheath was strapped inside the left sleeve of his shirt.

He'd first taken to wearing it back when he'd been one of the agents for Wright's detective agency. It had come in handy often enough to teach him the wisdom of continuing to wear it after he'd quit Wright's. For a man who now earned his way mostly with a deck of cards, the knife worked as a form of insurance.

Removing the blade, he got out of the rest of his

8   *L. W. Rogers*

clothes and slammed them against a post until he'd knocked off most of the hard-caked dust. He hunkered down inside the barrel, letting the cool water settle over his shoulders. After washing himself, he soaked the clothes in the barrel and wrung them out. Then he removed his town clothes from his saddlebags. After he dressed, he carried the wet clothes out of the barn and spread them on a humped rock to dry in the sun.

When he entered the log shack, the three men around the table stared at him. He didn't look like the same man. He wore black, relieved only by a gold cravat setting off the darkness of his linen shirt and the bone grip of his holstered Colt. His flat-crowned Stetson was an expensive one, and the broadcloth of his trousers and open frock coat had obviously been cut to measure by a good tailor.

As Driscoll sized up the man, he quickly revised his original estimate of Logan. Whatever the stranger was, he wasn't any ordinary cowpoke. Clothes like that meant money, and Driscoll prided himself on his poker skill. He used his boyish grin on the tall man. "Want to sit in? Pass the time 'til the stage comes."

"Good a way as any," Logan agreed and took the only empty chair across the table from the burly Bowles.

Little more than a half hour later, Bowles and the station manager were out of the game, broke. Plainly disgusted, they sat in their chairs as the game became a two-man duel. Over the stretch of played hands Driscoll had won most often, but Logan had raked in the biggest pots. The young redhead concentrated on reversing this

The Twisted Trail 9

trend, without success. Five deals later, the largest part of the money on the table sat in front of Logan.

Driscoll no longer smiled. He watched narrow-eyed as Logan dealt, noting how the cards, flicked out with apparent carelessness by the long, rope-scarred fingers, fell exactly into place one on top of the other. His eyes remained on Logan as he picked up the cards dealt to him.

"I've sure been dumb." He spoke his words through clenched teeth.

"No," Logan said. "You play a smart game. It's just the way the cards are running."

"I mean I sized you up wrong, Mister." Driscoll snapped out the words. "You're a gambler, ain't you?"

"I've played my share of poker," Logan conceded with a faint smile.

He'd been winning because he'd found Driscoll easy to read. Now he waited for the redhead to lose his temper and sensed he was close to it. After a glance at his cards, Driscoll simmered down. "I'll open for ten dollars." Which meant he held a hand strong enough to check his growing anger.

Logan's hand consisted of a pair of sixes, a pair of queens, and a nine. He saw the ten-dollar bet, not raising, and discarded the nine. Driscoll also threw away one card, but Logan decided it would require more than two pairs to control Driscoll's temper.

He dealt Driscoll a card, picked off one for himself; a jack didn't improve his two pairs at all. He watched Driscoll studying his own cards, making a show of having difficulty deciding how to play them.

10 *L. W. Rogers*

Finally Driscoll shrugged. "Might's well give you the rest of my dough." He shoved all of his remaining cash to the center of the table with the original twenty.

"'Fraid you've got me beat." Without expression, Logan folded his hand.

Fury showed on Driscoll's face. He'd held three kings to start with, had kept an ace and acquired another for a full house. And all it had earned him was ten dollars from Logan. With an effort, he forced a grin. "You bluff easy, gent."

"Oh?" Logan pretended innocence. "Were you bluffing?"

"Yeah."

"Joke's on me then. Your deal."

Driscoll raked in the pot and started shuffling the cards. This time Logan held only a pair of jacks. He opened for ten dollars. Driscoll took advantage by seeing Logan and raising another ten dollars, still forcing a grin.

Logan read Driscoll's face and played into the red-head's hand. Without a moment's hesitation, Driscoll saw the bet and raised it with everything he had left. His grin seemed pasted on his face now. Logan studied him, then counted the cash from his own pile and dropped it on the pot. "See you."

Driscoll's grin crumpled. He flung his cards on the table, faceup, showing only a pair of tens. Logan spread out his own cards and readied himself for an explosion.

The explosion didn't come. From outside, the sound of an approaching horse defused the tension. Driscoll turned and looked toward the open doorway.

The Twisted Trail 11

The station manager rose to his feet and lumbered to the door. "Go for days without company. Looks like this is my day not to be lonely."

Driscoll left his chair and walked to the window. "Man on a spotted horse." He turned to face the interior of the room again. His hand blurred, sweeping the gun out of his holster.

Logan saw the beginning of the move and went for his own gun. He didn't get a chance to find out if he'd have beaten the redhead to the draw. Bowles shoved his heavy bulk against the table, ramming it into Logan, and overturning him from his chair. Logan hit the floor hard, twisted, and came up on one knee, gripping the butt of his Colt. By then Driscoll held a dead aim on him, and Bowles had drawn his own revolver.

Logan opened his fingers, letting the Colt slide back into the holster as he rose to his feet. The station manager backed against the inside wall, stuttering, "W-what's this all 'bout?" Though he'd asked the question, he knew what it was. He already held his hands up, making no effort to go for his own gun.

Bowles relieved him of it and kept both pistols steady on Logan as Driscoll moved around behind the tall gambler and took his Colt. He shoved the weapon into his own belt.

The leathery-faced Munoz appeared in the doorway. "Stage coming."

"How much time we have?"

"Ten minutes . . . mebbe less," Munoz guessed.

Driscoll nodded without taking his eyes from Logan.

12 *L. W. Rogers*

"Get all the horses inside the barn. Then stay out of sight and cover from there."

As Munoz vanished, Driscoll stepped to the table. He pointed his pistol toward Logan and the station manager. With his free hand he began picking up the money and stuffing it into his pockets. "Looks like I win after all, gambler."

Logan matched Driscoll's stare without expression.

Driscoll pocketed the last of Logan's winnings. "Mebbe you figure it belongs to you? I say you were cheatin', tinhorn."

Logan merely continued looking wooden-faced at Driscoll. His failure to show any reaction enraged Driscoll. With a vicious tightening of his face, the redhead slammed the barrel of his gun at Logan's head.

Logan moved as the heavy gun barrel caught him in the temple. He saved himself from the full force of the blow, which still had enough to drop him to the floor with his senses spinning and pain lashing through his brain.

"Get over by the window," Driscoll snapped at Bowles. While the heavy man obeyed, Driscoll broke open the station manager's gun and dumped all the cartridges. He closed the revolver, went to the manager, and shoved it back in his holster. "Now when the stagecoach pulls up, you go out there and act like nothing's wrong. Savvy?"

The station manager nodded quickly and tried to speak, but found his voice had left him.

"You better." Driscoll's voice held a deadly threat. " 'Less you want your spine broke by a bullet."

The Twisted Trail 13

"We oughta kill him and the gambler now," Bowles said. "Make the job that much easier when the stage—"

"You seem to forget that I'm runnin' this show." Driscoll snarled. "And I say we'll wait and make sure Denham's on that stage first. If he ain't, there's no point in killing anybody else. Having the law on our tail for murder is one thing. Without gettin' paid for it is something I ain't willing to do."

Logan remained sprawled on the floor with his shoulders against the wall, fighting against dizziness and the blurring of his vision. The sound of the approaching stagecoach reached him. He raised his right hand and gently touched the swollen bruise on the side of his head. He let his hand fall so that its fingers touched the cuff of his left sleeve.

Neither Driscoll nor Bowles saw anything in the motion to alarm them.

Chapter Two

The plump station manager came out of the log shack as the stage pulled to a jangling, screeching halt in front of it. His empty gun in his holster, his hands hung akimbo at his sides, he tried his best to smile as ordered. Except he moved as though he were stepping on eggs.

The big man riding shotgun up beside the team driver raised a hand in greeting. "Howdy, Percy. How late are we?"

The station manager worked his throat open to get the words out. "'Bout an hour." He lost his struggle to keep the smile on his face. Although he desired to break through his fear, to shout a warning and throw himself to the ground, the massive awareness of the two men hidden inside the shack with guns aimed at his back outweighed his need.

The Twisted Trail   15

Numbly he watched the driver lock the brake and tie the reins, saw the coach door open and the three passengers, all men, climb out to stretch their legs.

Driscoll came out of the doorway behind the station manager. Bowles appeared inside the window, dividing his attention between Logan and the men outside, ready to turn his gun in either direction, as needed. Logan braced his heavy shoulders against the wall and waited, his head lolling to one side as though he were still semi-conscious. The mist in front of his eyes began to dissolve and the tips of his fingers were now inside the left sleeve of his coat.

Outside, Driscoll shoved the station manager out of his way and smiled at one particular passenger who climbed out of the coach—a middle-aged businessman.

"Howdy, Denham."

Henry Denham recognized Driscoll at once. The moment Denham spotted the gun in Driscoll's hand he knew what was coming, and he reached to the inside pocket of his jacket where he kept a derringer.

Driscoll laughed softly and the gun in his hand roared. The slug rammed into Denham's chest, driving him back against the coach and pinning him there for a split second. As he crumpled toward the ground, the man riding shotgun atop the stage broke out of his stupor and twisted in his high seat, bringing his rifle around to take a bead on the red-haired killer.

Before he could squeeze the trigger, Munoz's rifle sounded from inside the barn. The bullet caught the stage guard in the head, killing him instantly. His rifle

16 *L. W. Rogers*

spilled from lifeless hands and fell as he sagged back in the high seat next to the stage driver.

The team horses, frightened by the crash of gunfire, reared and whinnied. The driver reached forward and grabbed the reins to hold the animals steady. The other two passengers had already thrown their hands high and stood frozen, eager to give no one an excuse to shoot at them.

It was all over in the blink of an eye. Or it seemed to be. Driscoll stood holding his Colt carelessly, gazing down at the still figure of Denham in the dust. Munoz walked from the barn toward the shack, rifle still ready in both hands.

Inside the shack Bowles turned his attention from Logan and called through the window to Driscoll. "Might's well lift whatever the passengers got on 'em while we're—"

Logan came to life in the same instant, drawing the knife out of his sleeve and throwing it in one motion as he lunged to his feet.

Bowles whipped around, trying to shoot Logan and dodge the flung knife at the same time. He succeeded in neither. The knife blade plunged deep into his throat, cutting off his scream. He squeezed the trigger automatically as he fell forward. The gun boomed within the confines of the small room, the slug chopping into the wooden wall.

Logan reached Bowles as his body hit the dirt floor. Snatching his own Colt from the dead man's belt, he straightened beside the window, ready to fire through it at Driscoll.

The Twisted Trail   17

The redhead reacted fast to the sound of the shot inside the shack. By the time Logan reached the window, Driscoll had grabbed one of the passengers to use as a shield, keeping the man between himself and the shack. He'd accomplished his mission by killing Denham and saw no reason for a shootout. His only concern now was to get away alive.

It seemed Munoz, who stood halfway between the barn and the shack, had a different idea. He'd spotted Logan and decided to get him. He brought the rifle to his shoulder and took aim at the window. As he fired, Logan took a step backward, deeper into the shadows. The rifle's bullet whizzed past his ear as he aimed and fired his revolver. In spite of the distance, the slug got Munoz in the hip, staggering him, but he didn't go down.

Logan took aim again. Another shot sounded, this time from next to the stagecoach. The plump station manager had lowered to one knee and grabbed the rifle dropped by the dead guard. It was his bullet that stopped Munoz.

While the rifle shot still echoed, Driscoll fired from behind his human shield. The station master fell back with a scream of pain, clutching his shoulder. Driscoll continued backing toward the barn, one hand gripping the back of his prisoner's coat, too well hidden behind the other man for Logan to try a shot.

In two quick steps, Logan moved from the window to the door. He slid his revolver back into its holster, crouched low, and dodged out toward the rifle the wounded station master had dropped. Driscoll's bullet kicked dirt against his leg as he reached and grabbed for

18   *L. W. Rogers*

the weapon. Logan dodged back to the protection of the corner of the log shack.

"Anyone try to stop me," Driscoll yelled, "and I shoot this pilgrim in the head."

Logan levered a fresh shell into the rifle's chamber and aimed, hoping the man being used as a shield would have the good sense to drop out of the way. One good shot at the redhead's chest is all he needed. Such wasn't the case. The passenger's face was blank with shock and terror. His big figure continued to block Driscoll from view the rest of the way to the barn.

Logan stayed where he was, waiting to get a shot at Driscoll when he left the barn. Two shots sounded inside the barn. Seconds later two horses raced out of the other end of the barn, headed for the hills to the north. Driscoll rode one horse and led the other. And he had his hostage up on the first horse clinging to his back, still shielding him.

"Dang!" Logan swore aloud as he sprinted to the barn. Inside he found what he'd expected. Driscoll had shot the other two horses in the corral.

Coming out of the barn, he watched Driscoll riding fast up the nearest hill. At the top, without stopping, the red-haired killer turned in his saddle and clubbed his gun against his hostage's head. The man fell backward from the horse and rolled partway down the slope. Before Logan could fire, Driscoll and his two horses disappeared down the other side of the hill.

Logan lowered his rifle and glanced toward the stage and the shack. The station master leaned against the

The Twisted Trail 19

wall, and the remaining passenger was trying to do what he could for the plump man's shoulder wound. It surprised Logan to see the stagecoach driver sitting on the ground with Denham's head on his lap.

Hurrying to them, he saw that Denham wasn't dead, though he was getting closer to it by the second. His blood-smeared chest heaved weakly and a death glaze covered his eyes. Pink froth bubbled between his white lips as he tried to speak.

"What's he saying?" Logan asked the stage driver.

"Cain't make it out. Something about hired killers is all I got so far."

Logan knelt over the dying man. "Do you know who hired them?"

Denham made an effort to answer. Broken, unintelligible sounds came out of him.

Logan bent closer. "Who hired those men to kill you? Do you know?"

Denham's lips twisted as he tried to get the words out. The only ones Logan understood were, "bastard . . . said . . . he'd stop me . . ."

"Who?" Logan repeated.

This time no answer of any kind came. Denham stopped making the effort. His head rolled against the stage driver's knee and was still. He'd finished his dying.

Logan stood up and trudged out to the unconscious man on the side of the hill.

Chapter Three

The stagecoach took six hours to reach Fort Brooke. On the way Logan rode up beside the driver and learned what he knew about Henry Denham. Logan's interest was strictly personal. The red-haired killer had robbed him of his stake and his winnings and pistol-whipped him in the bargain. These were things for which Logan would seek retribution. About such matters Logan had the persistence and patience of his grandfather's Creek Indian blood. He figured the best method of finding the redhead was through whoever had hired him to do the killing.

"You got any notion who'd want Denham dead?"

The stage driver clucked to the team of horses. "Cain't rightly say. I do know Denham ran a freight line out of Fort Brooke. Seems he'd hit a string of bad luck

The Twisted Trail 21

and near 'bout ready to go out of business when he'd acquired a new partner recently who'd poured fresh money into his business."

Logan listened with interest. "Was he a bad business man?"

"Don't think so. The way I heard it, Denham had sunk all his profits into a big cattle ranch down on the Okeechobee and hadn't been able to weather his business losses on his own."

Logan braced a hand against the side of the seat when the coach hit a deep rut. "That don't seem like much of a reason to kill a man."

"Gee-up there, hoss," the driver shouted to the team to get the horses up a sandy grade. After the coach leveled out, he turned his attention back to Logan. "Don't know 'bout that. Only know Denham had taken on a partner who'd sunk quite a bit of money into his freight company."

"How about this new partner of his?"

The driver shook his head. "Remember when he was trying to tell us who hired them? He said the *bastard* hired 'em. Never heard nobody call a woman that before. Some get called a lot of other things, but not that."

"Denham's partner is a woman?"

"Uh-huh. Don't know much about her 'cept she's mighty good-looking. Makes you sweat just to look at her. She ain't from anywhere 'round here. Name's Clarissa Hubbard."

The woman's name brought back a flash of memory.

22 *L. W. Rogers*

He wondered if she was the beautiful, sassy gambler down Mississippi way? She was the kind of woman who could give a man an eternal itch.

Logan leaned against the hard, jouncing seat, gazing thoughtfully past the pulling horses, across the flat distances to the southern horizon. He dismissed the thought as a mere coincidence that there might be two women sharing the name Clarissa Hubbard.

Night had settled in when the stage rolled into Fort Brooke, a sprawling frontier boomtown that cut through to the bay. For a couple of years it had been the worst hell-spot in the Territory. Now its lawless period was past, ended by a town-taming marshal named Brody.

Still a wild enough place, Fort Brooke's red-light district flourished. Marshal Brody, his tough-reputationed deputies, and a sheriff strong enough to handle the surrounding county kept the wildness under rigid control, confining the red-light goings-on to an allotted section of town.

Within minutes of stepping off the stagecoach, Logan had met the marshal and the sheriff. Both lived up to their reputations for efficiency. The wounded station master was immediately turned over to a doctor, the bodies of the shotgun rider and Henry Denham to the undertaker. The two passengers, one with a sizeable lump on his head, were questioned and allowed to register into the hotel. Twenty minutes after the stage rolled in, the sheriff rode out with a posse of six hand-picked men to hunt down the red-haired killer.

Logan didn't give the posse good odds of finding

The Twisted Trail 23

Driscoll, especially since they weren't able to start tracking until dawn. With that much head start and two horses for speed, Logan knew Driscoll could get beyond the sheriff's jurisdiction before the posse got anywhere near him. He'd been heading northwest the last time Logan had seen him. That way lay Indian territory and land that still had no law. All Driscoll had to do was keep on going.

While Marshal Brody went off to talk to Denham's partner, one of his deputies took Logan and the stage driver to the jailhouse office. They looked at a stack of wanted posters, searching the faces of desperadoes— men wanted from all over the southwest during the past couple of years.

They finished going through the stack, unable to spot any picture or description that fit the red-haired killer, by the time Marshal Brody returned. Brody was a big, raw-boned man with a pockmarked face, dominated by the kind of eyes to be expected in a man who'd tamed four hell-towns over the past ten years.

"Any luck?" he asked in a friendly tone that didn't quite go with his eyes.

His deputy shook his head. "Clarissa Hubbard have any notion who the redhead is?"

"Nope. Nor who hired him, she says."

"Somebody," Logan said in a quiet voice, "must have some ideas about it."

Marshal Brody eyed him thoughtfully for a moment, sizing him up. "Sure, people have got suspicions. Lots of 'em, all going in different directions and not worth

24 *L. W. Rogers*

a tinker's damn. I got a couple myself. Both of which are probably wrong."

"I'd like to hear them anyway."

The marshal sat down in his wooden chair and propped his boots on top of the desk. He leaned back, his hands braced behind his head. "Suspicions aren't proof. Making accusations without proof's against the law."

The stage driver spoke up. "Can I go now, Marshal? I ain't needed a drink so bad in a long time."

Brody nodded. The driver unbuckled his gunbelt and left it on the desk. As he hurried out, the marshal turned to Logan.

"I'll take yours too. Only lawmen are allowed to tote weapons in Fort Brooke."

"You must have a real peaceful town."

Brody grunted. "Haven't had a quiet night since I came here. Men got a right to let off steam, long as they do it in the right part of town. I don't care what they do to each other with their fists, boots or anything else they can get hold of, long as it doesn't start a riot or break up too much property. But weapons mean killing. And killing usually means the town has to pay for the burial. Taxpayers don't like that."

Logan contemplated the consequences of not handing over his weapons. Eventually he unbuckled his gun belt and laid it alongside his carbine on the marshal's desk.

Brody went on eyeing him. "The rules also include knives, Logan." He kept his tone deliberately quiet, as he didn't intend to give offense. His past ten years testified

The Twisted Trail 25

to his readiness to stand up against all kinds of men. It also testified to his ability to judge men. He'd already decided that Logan wasn't the kind of man he'd care to tangle with, unless forced to it.

"Reckon those men that were after Denham thought they'd disarmed you," he went on quietly. "And you surprised 'em when you came up with a knife from someplace."

"I hope," the quietness in Logan's voice matched Brody's, "that you're this careful about everybody who comes into your city."

Marshal Brody nodded. "I got a collection of derringers and knives in that closet to prove it. Nobody fancies thirty days in the quarry digging rock for the new town hall. And that's the penalty for carrying any concealed weapon inside city limits. Penalty for using one is hanging."

"Hung many?"

"Some. None lately, though."

A suggestion of a smile touched the corners of Logan's mouth. He pulled up the left sleeve of his frock coat, unbuttoned and rolled up his shirt sleeve.

The marshal looked at the knife strapped in its sheath to the inside of Logan's forearm, hilt toward his wrist, "So that's where you had it."

Logan unstrapped the knife and put it down beside his holstered Colt. "I may be back for the guns. If I find somebody that'll pay me enough for them to last through a few hands of poker. That red-haired varmit just about cleaned me out."

26 *L. W. Rogers*

"In the meantime, you'll probably want to eat," Brody said. "You can get a meal at the City Diner, around the corner. Tell 'em I said to put it on my bill. I figure you earned it out there at the stage station."

"Thanks. Where can I find Clarissa Hubbard?"

"Hillsboro Hotel. Up the street." Marshal Brody indicated the direction with his thumb. He asked no questions about why Logan wanted to know. His eyes were thoughtful again as they watched him out of the jailhouse and up the street.

The Hillsboro Hotel was the best in prosperous Fort Brooke. Logan stepped through the double doors into the plush red carpeted lobby. Long strides took him to where the desk clerk stood behind an ornate mahogany counter with a gold foot rail spanning the length of the counter.

"Is Clarissa Hubbard in her room?"

With a look of disdain at Logan's dusty attire, the young clerk dressed in a red and white pinstriped shirt said, "Miss Hubbard has just gone into the hotel dining room."

Logan turned toward the dining room. "Thanks."

"Excuse me sir, but—"

"But what?" Logan didn't like it when the clerk stepped in front of him as if to block his way.

"You're not dressed—" the young clerk seemed to shrink under Logan's dark stare.

Logan merely harrumphed, stepped around the clerk, and headed toward the dining room. He spotted Clarissa

The Twisted Trail 27

Hubbard alone at one of the corner tables, studying a menu.

Though he'd only seen her once before, she was exactly as he remembered. Clarissa Hubbard wasn't a woman a man could easily forget. She wore her black hair piled high on her head with ringlets hanging down the back of her neck. Her lips were full and beautiful. She was bold and knowing, with a sensuous kind of loveliness. There was a strength in the assured way in which she held herself and moved. Only her dress was different from the last time he'd seen her. The one she wore now looked like a French import. Cut modestly enough, the material with its navy-blue darkness clung softly to her curves, flaunting them. She had a figure that didn't need much help at flaunting itself.

Clarissa looked up as he approached her table. Lustrous almond-shaped eyes took in his measure and found him interesting.

Logan took off his black hat. "Good evening, Miss Hubbard. My name's Matt Logan. I was around when your partner got himself killed."

Her interest in him became more definite. "The marshal told me about you. That was quite a thing you did." She lowered her eyes, then slowly looked up at him again. "Won't you join me for dinner?" With a brief sweep of her hand, she indicated the chair next to hers.

Logan shifted on one foot. He fingered the brim of his hat. "Like to, ma'am. I'm a bit short on cash."

"My treat then. Or would a woman buying you a meal offend your manliness?"

28 *L. W. Rogers*

Her comment caused Logan to chuckle. "Don't know about my manliness, but my stomach wouldn't mind at all."

As he seated himself across the table from her a waiter came over. Clarissa placed her order and passed the menu to Logan. She studied him as he ordered. When the waiter was gone she said, "Marshal Brody thinks you're a gambler. Are you?"

He nodded. "And how have the cards been running for you lately?"

She leaned back a little in her chair, surprised. "You know me from some place?"

"I saw you once a couple of years back on a riverboat in Mississippi, backing the biggest poker game in the place." He smiled at her. "As I recall, you were winning pretty steadily."

Her beautifully curved lips quirked. "I usually manage to win more than I lose."

"Uh-huh. A good-looking woman is a natural draw for the big-money suckers."

She smiled at him more fully. "So we're both in the same line of business. How nice."

"I heard you'd changed your line. Gone into freighting."

"That's strictly a one-time thing. Henry Denham made me a proposition too good to pass up." Her face clouded as she spoke of her dead partner. "I've got almost every cent I've saved invested in a shipment coming in by boat from Jacksonville tomorrow. That was

The Twisted Trail   29

our deal. My money and Denham's wagons, mule teams and know-how. Equal shares in the profits."

"How does the deal stand with Denham dead?" Out of respect for the deceased, Logan kept his voice low.

"The same. Except that it's going to be harder without him."

"And the profits? What about them?"

Clarissa stiffened just a bit. "I was to get half. That hasn't changed. Only now Denham's share goes to his family."

Logan sat silent. His blue eyes searched her face.

She met his gaze directly. "That's one thing I never cheat on, Logan. I always pay what I owe."

"No offense meant, ma'am." Logan liked the passion in her eyes when she'd snapped out her answer.

"None taken." Clarissa lifted a brow. She reached for her coffee cup and sipped calmly.

The waiter brought their food. Over the meal she told Logan about how she'd met Henry Denham in Mississippi. He'd gone there trying to buy a big shipment of freight on credit, without success. A mutual acquaintance, a big cattle buyer who didn't seem to mind having lost a considerable amount to her over the poker table, introduced them. Denham loosened up with her more than he might have with a man. He'd told her of the plan he had for recouping his business losses, if he could only get his hands on a big shipment of supplies.

"What kind of supplies?" Logan regarded Clarissa with interest.

30 *L. W. Rogers*

"Oh, things like barrels of flour, salted meat, soap, clothing, whiskey . . ." Clarissa met his stare.

She related how Denham had just come from Atlanta. Shortly before he'd left, there'd been a big gold strike farther north in the mountains. He told how miners were pouring into a place called Dahlonega by the hundreds, and that the place was a makeshift miners' camp and short of supplies. He'd also explained how it was already beginning to snow up there. In another few weeks, more or less, Dahlonega would be snowed in, making it next to impossible to get freight wagons through to it.

"Anybody getting there with supplies before the snow blocks the way will make a fortune. Every item brought in will bring twenty times its worth, in gold."

Logan watched the animated way her eyes danced while she explained her part in the deal with Denham.

With that kind of payoff as a reward, Denham hadn't had to do much persuading to get Clarissa Hubbard to sink her money into the venture as his partner.

"Outside of his cash shortage, he apparently had no troubles with anyone." Clarissa lifted her coffee cup and sipped.

"He had trouble, all right," Logan said. "Trouble worth killing over."

"None that he told me about."

"He could've been afraid to. Afraid you'd pull out of your deal with him."

"If so, he misjudged me. I've played some risky games before and for smaller profits. I'd have stuck. No matter what."

The Twisted Trail 31

Logan guessed that she would have. For sure, under that soft provocative exterior, there was steel in her.

"Without Denham, who're you planning to have take your freight wagons through to Dahlonega for you?"

She seemed to consider his question and took her time answering. "I'm taking them through myself. With men I'll hire to follow my orders."

"That's a rough trail for a woman," Logan told her. "You'll have a stretch of marshlands, a few sand dunes, and once in the mountains, well . . . that won't be any picnic either. I've been up that way. Once you get your wagons through those Georgia hills, then there's Bull Mountain in Dahlonega. At eighteen hundred feet, it's smaller than most mountains along the Appalachian range."

"What about the snow? Does it get as deep as Tennessee?"

Logan cut a sizeable chunk of steak and chewed appreciatively before answering. He rested his arms on the edge of the table. "It isn't the snow you have to worry about, Clarissa. The white stuff only sticks for a few days. When it melts, the cold turns it to ice. Then when the ice melts, all that red clay turns to gumbo. Makes it difficult for even the heartiest mule teams to pull freight-loaded wagons up thirty miles of single track."

Clarissa peered at him over the rim of her demitasse cup. Was he trying to discourage her?

"I know all about that. I'm going. Just as I intended to from the start."

32 *L. W. Rogers*

"Even when Denham was alive to take the wagons up?"

"That's right. Denham was a family man, a decent sort. I trusted him." She seemed to think for a moment. "I've never trusted anyone that much. Those supplies are going to trade for an awful lot of nuggets. I intend to be there to keep count when the gold is paid over."

The conversation ended. Logan and Clarissa concentrated on their steaks and fried potatoes. They were finishing the meal when a man entered the dining room, glanced around, and then walked straight toward their table. A stocky, well-dressed, cold-eyed man in his early forties, with thinning gray hair and a cleft chin that accented his handsome face.

Logan remembered seeing him in the crowd that had gathered when the stage pulled into Fort Brooke.

Behind him and a little to one side trailed two other men, not so well dressed. Logan had never seen either before but he knew the look and the manner. He figured them for bodyguards. One was built like a brick house with beefy hands and a face that looked as if it had been scrambled by several blows from a sledgehammer sometime in his past.

The other was a slim, surly-faced kid who kept brushing the fingertips of his right hand over his thigh as he moved, as if he missed the feel of the gun he'd ordinarily be packing there.

The well-dressed man in the lead stopped at the table where Logan and Clarissa sat, his cold eyes flicking over Logan to settle on Clarissa.

The Twisted Trail   33

"Miss Hubbard. I haven't had the pleasure of an introduction, so may I introduce myself? My name's Sullivan, Carl Sullivan."

Watching Clarissa's lack of expression as she sized Sullivan up, Logan saw part of the reason for her success as a gambler.

"How do you know who I am?" she asked, nothing in her voice but natural curiosity.

"You were pointed out to me earlier today."

"Pointed out?" Her eyebrows arched a bit. "For what reason?"

"A pretty woman interests everyone." Although he smiled at her, there was nothing warm in the depths of his eyes. "I have a business proposition for you," he went on smoothly. "May I sit down?"

"Of course. Business offers are something I'm always willing to listen to."

Sullivan pulled out one of the chairs from the table, giving his full attention to her. His bodyguards stood a short distance away, their eyes on Logan.

"I'm sorry to hear about your partner," Sullivan said. "I knew Henry Denham slightly. Met up with him in North Georgia. As a matter of fact, it seems both of us got the same idea after the gold strike, you know, the idea of taking supplies into Dahlonega before the snows close the way. I also have a shipment coming in by way of boat tomorrow afternoon. And I have wagons ready to carry the goods."

Sullivan paused and hunched forward a little on his chair, his face earnest. "Miss Hubbard, with Denham

34 *L. W. Rogers*

dead and unable to take your wagons into the gold fields, you're stuck with all those supplies you paid for. I'm prepared to take those supplies from you. I'll pay what you paid for them . . . plus a tidy profit."

Logan leaned back in his chair, forcing his shoulders to relax against the tension building inside him.

Clarissa offered Sullivan a thin smile. "Fort Brooke-type profit, Mr. Sullivan? Or Dahlonega-sized profit?"

Sullivan fashioned another smile for her. "We're in Fort Brooke. It's right here I'd be buying. I'll pay you what the goods are worth here and another hundred to make it worthwhile selling to me rather than any of the general stores in town."

Clarissa returned Sullivan's smile. "Those supplies are worth twenty times that much in Dahlonega and you know it."

Sullivan moved his hand impatiently, as though brushing aside her statement. "My offer is your only way out financially. Unless, of course, you plan to hire some man to take Denham's place in getting your freight to the gold fields. And I advise you strongly against trusting anyone that far. Mighty big temptation."

"I don't intend to, Mr. Sullivan. *I'm* taking my shipment to Dahlonega."

Sullivan shot Clarissa a withering look. A deep line of concentration dug itself between his eyes. "Being a little foolish aren't you? You, a lone woman with the rough sort of men needed to handle the wagons, a long way from civilization . . ." He let the sentence dangle.

The Twisted Trail   35

"I own a gun." Clarissa's voice was as cold as the grease on her plate. "And I know how to use it. I've taken care of myself in the uncivilized world for a long time."

"You worry me, Miss Hubbard—"

"I bet she does," Logan cut in softly. "And so did Denham."

Sullivan's cold eyes fastened on the man seated next to Clarissa. His voice sounded dry as leaves when he said, "What do you mean by that?"

Logan's hard, cynical eyes stared back at Sullivan. "Two separate wagon trains getting to Dahlonega about the same time would cut into your profits. There'd be twice as many supplies, cutting down the worth of each item. With the people there having a choice of who to buy from, you couldn't hold out for the kind of profits you'd like. You'll make even less if she gets to Dahlonega ahead of you. Her supplies would be all sold by the time you got there. That mean's you'd have to sell to slightly less-anxious customers."

Sullivan thrummed his fingers against the white linen tablecloth. He matched Logan's stare. "That's a consideration, of course. I didn't claim to offer the lady charity."

Logan's mouth twisted derisively. Mockery crept into his voice. "What did you offer Denham, up there in the gold fields? Maybe you just warned him. Warned him that if he tried competing with you, you'd find a way to stop him."

One of the bodyguards stepped toward Logan. Sullivan stopped the man with a quick gesture. He and Logan continued to stare at each other. Then Sullivan turned back to Clarissa.

"I made you a fair offer," he said, his manner now abrupt. The words came out clipped and hard. "You'd be wise to accept it. As I told you, it's a long haul to Dahlonega, through bad country. Anything could happen to you along the way." He let a faint hint of a threat leak into his voice. Not much, just enough to be felt.

She continued to smile at him, unmoved. "Thanks for telling me. I like to know the rules before I sit in on a game."

"This is no game, Miss Hubbard. It could be very dangerous for you—even fatal." Sullivan stood up. "Think it over carefully. You have time . . . until the ship arrives tomorrow afternoon." He placed his hands on the table, splayed his fingers, and leaned toward Clarissa. "I won't repeat my offer. You can come to me anytime you decide to accept it. I'm in room nineteen, in this hotel."

He turned and walked away without another glance at Logan.

His two bodyguards went on staring at Logan for a moment before they turned and followed Sullivan.

Chapter Four

Clarissa Hubbard dropped her smile as she looked at Logan. "You think he's the one who paid to have Denham killed?"

"Smells that way." His blue eyes watched her. "Any chance of your taking Sullivan's offer?"

"Not a chance in the world. If he wants to make it a race to Dahlonega, I'll give it to him."

"He'll do more than race you. He'll try every dirty trick in the book to stop you."

She nodded, frowning. "He made that clear enough."

"You'll need a man to take Denham's place as wagon master. I can see your point in wanting to make this trip, wanting to make sure you're not cheated. Reckon, though, it'll take a man to run things on the trail, make no mistake about that."

38   *L. W. Rogers*

She eyed him calculatingly. "Sounds almost like you want the job yourself."

"I do."

"Why?" Her voice was wary.

Logan's lips thinned. "There's a man I want to meet again. He's likely to show up wherever Sullivan needs another killing job done for him."

"That young redhead Marshal Brody mentioned?"

"Uh-huh."

She thought about the story the marshal had told her of what Logan had done at the stage station. She knew how to read men. She'd learned across a lot of poker tables and in a number of situations that hadn't had anything to do with gambling. She'd already sized up Matt Logan.

First there were certain practical considerations she had to make. "Being captain of a wagon train requires experience." She cocked an eyebrow as if she were issuing a challenge. "You have experience?"

"I have it." He kept his voice flat. "Ran a few supply trains through the posts in Arizona territory when I was scouting for the army. Don't worry. I can handle the job."

"Arizona, huh? Hmm. Long way from Florida." Though she regarded him with surprise, Clarissa gave him an appreciative look. "Gambler, army scout, wagon master. Hmm. Seems you're a jack-of-all-trades. Anything else to add to your list of jobs?"

"That's about it." Logan shrugged. "I get restless."

"You a married man, Logan?" Clarissa surprised

The Twisted Trail 39

herself by asking the question. "Wouldn't want you to get a sudden itch to go visit the wife and leave me high and dry before getting my goods to Dahlonega."

When his blue eyes darkened and took on a far away sadness, Clarissa realized, in an instant, she'd intruded on forbidden territory.

He was quiet for a moment and when he spoke his voice was husky and succinct. "Was once. Buried my wife and baby girl, long time ago."

Clarissa studied his handsome face, etched with lines of sorrow. She sighed. "Forgive me. I had no right to intrude."

He caught and held her gaze. "Do I have the job or not?"

She tapped a bright red fingernail against her cheek as if trying to make up her mind. "All right. The job's yours."

"Good." Logan's face remained serious. "How many wagons have you got?"

"Eight."

"How many men to drive them?"

"I've got six teamsters. Men who were loyal to Henry Denham. All good men."

"That leaves us short two."

Clarissa glanced around the room, then back at Logan. "In the morning you can help me hire the other two."

"If those two men Sullivan had with him are samples of his crew," Logan said, "it'll take more than mule skinners to get your wagons through. We'll need some men to ride guard. The right kind of men, if you get my drift."

40 *L. W. Rogers*

Clarissa nodded. She thought about Carl Sullivan, his business proposition, and his veiled threat. Though she didn't scare easily, she was never one to overplay her cards. "I've been giving that some thought."

"Anyone in mind?"

"Not yet. Henry and I never found ourselves in need of ruffians."

"All right, then. I'll search around and see what I can find."

Clarissa leaned forward and placed her hand on Logan's arm. The look she gave him was all business. "Subject to my approval."

"Fair enough, boss lady."

They talked money. She didn't have much left and the wages she could offer were not exceptional. She would compensate with a hefty bonus to each man after the freight was sold in Dahlonega.

Logan interrupted her reverie. "I'll need an advance on my wages."

Clarissa opened the handbag on her lap, counted out fifty dollars onto the table. "Enough?"

"It'll do. Care to play some poker?"

An hour later in her room on the top floor of the hotel, Logan pushed the last of the fifty dollars she'd advanced him across the table to her.

"You play mighty slick poker for a lady." Nothing in his face or voice betrayed that he'd discovered the tiny notches on the brand new cards, where she'd marked them with her thumb while dealing.

The Twisted Trail

"I've had a lot of practice," she said, with a touch of humor in her greenish eyes.

A corner of Logan's mouth quirked. "And your looking good enough to eat helps too. Takes a man's mind off the game." Her eyes reminded him of cat eyes; her ruby red lips, and the green and gold silk gown that bared her pale shoulders and décolleté had certainly taken his mind off the game. Usually he sat down to poker in a naturally suspicious frame of mind. Only the heady effect of her perfume and of being alone in the softly lit bedroom with her had kept him from feeling the markings on the cards for a long time.

She stretched like a cat, gave him a lazy smile, and fairly purred when she said, "A long time ago a riverboat gambler told me the same thing. It's what started me on my career. Are you quitting?"

"Only if you'll advance me another fifty dollars on my wages."

Clarissa shrugged. "It's your money." She pushed over the fifty she'd won from him. "This makes it a hundred dollars worth of wages I've advanced you."

Logan nodded. "At this rate you won't owe me anything but a good-bye drink when we reach Dahlonega."

Fifteen minutes later he'd memorized all her thumbnail notches. After that his fingertips were able to read the cards she'd marked as he dealt them. By the time she realized that he was not just having a phenomenal run of luck, he'd won back his wages plus thirty-two dollars of her money.

42 *L. W. Rogers*

She eyed him suspiciously as he showed three aces to beat her three kings. With an innocent smile, he raked in the pot.

Her laughter was soft and without malice. "Took you longer to catch on than I expected."

"You make it hard for a man to concentrate."

The way those blue eyes of his looked at her began to have an effect that surprised her. She kept her tone light. "I couldn't resist trying, just to find out what you're made of. I did warn you there was only one thing I don't cheat about."

Logan sat back in his chair and stretched. "You warned me. Now I know you meant it."

Clarissa stood up. "Well, now that we know a little more about each other, I think we should call it an evening. I want to be at my best tomorrow."

His eyes followed her for a moment. She moved with a pantherish grace that accentuated her sensual looks. He stood and walked to the window, closed the shutters, and locked them.

She watched him, head cocked a little to one side. "Hope you aren't planning to make yourself at home."

Logan masked the concern in his voice. "Just taking precautions. If it was Sullivan who had Denham killed, he might try stopping you next."

"Your concern is touching, but unnecessary. I do know how to take care of myself." Clarissa looked at his handsome face, bronzed from the sun and finely chiseled. His mouth strong—the lower lip fuller than the upper—

The Twisted Trail   43

above a chin that showed great determination. "Or were you thinking of guarding me all night?"

The way his mouth quirked into a grin and the way his eyes continued to look at her made her knees go weak. Logan didn't say a word for a moment. "I'd feel safer about you if you weren't spending the night alone."

There was a logic to what he said, but she refused to be kept under lock and key. "Ah-hmm, that's just a bit too fast for me, Logan." Her voice was low and seductive, but firm. "I don't know you that well."

Logan picked up his hat and walked to the door. "You will," he told her, and closed the door behind him.

He stood outside her room until he heard her lock the door from the inside.

Driscoll waited in the darkness of a stand of scrub oaks east of town. He sat on the hard earth leaning back against the trunk of a tree, studying the stars overhead while his two horses nibbled at the sparse grass under the branches. The faint sounds of men approaching on foot brought him swiftly to his feet, his fingertips automatically brushing the grip of his holstered Colt.

The figures of three men appeared through the starlit darkness. Carl Sullivan, flanked by the broad-faced bruiser and the slim kid. When they were close enough, Driscoll noted the men wore no guns, at least none that showed. He figured Sullivan hadn't wanted to attract attention to their slipping out of town by claiming their guns from the marshal's office.

44 *L. W. Rogers*

"Howdy, Mr. Sullivan," Driscoll greeted him. "Denham get into Fort Brooke all right?"

"He came in just fine, Driscoll. Exactly the way I wanted him—dead as a doornail."

"He caught on to who I was soon as he saw me. Must've remembered seeing us together up in Atlanta."

"I hear you had some trouble gettin' the job done."

Driscoll sniggered. "I didn't have any trouble at all. Bowles and Munoz did, though." He held out his left hand, palm up. "Pay-up time, Mr. Sullivan."

Sullivan drew the money from his pocket and handed it over. Driscoll counted it, then stuffed the bills down inside his pants pocket. He didn't take his eyes off Sullivan. "That's just two hundred. You promised six hundred."

"Six hundred for the three of you," Sullivan said. "That comes to two hundred apiece. You got your third, like I agreed."

"Uh-uh. You said six hundred for doin' the job. The job's been done. Ain't my fault Bowles and Munoz ain't around to share it with me." His voice held a nasty cutting edge to it. He shoved his left hand forward again. "Give."

Moose, the big bruiser on Sullivan's right, shifted his feet.

Driscoll snapped. "Don't go gittin' nervous, Peckerhead!" His hand slapped lightly against his holster. The sound froze the big man.

Sullivan waved the bodyguard aside. He reached into his other pocket and pulled out the rest of the money. "No hard feelings, friend." He placed the money in

The Twisted Trail 45

Driscoll's palm. "Besides, I may have more work for you, on the trail to Dahlonega."

"Sure . . . sure. I can always use more cash." Driscoll sucked the air between a gap in his front teeth.

"Then hole up at Fish Eatn' Creek and wait for me. I'll bring the freight up through there day after tomorrow."

"I'll be there." Driscoll pocketed the money and untethered his horses, watching Sullivan's bodyguards while he did so.

"Be careful," Sullivan told him. "Sheriff's out with a posse hunting for you."

"They'll play hell tryin' to follow the trail I left." Driscoll swung up onto his saddle, tugged the other horse by the lead rope, and rode off into the darkness.

Scudder, the thin, surly kid with Sullivan said, "He don't look so tough to me. If'n I'd had my gun, you wouldn't have had to pay him the rest of that dough."

Sullivan harrumphed. "You've never seen Driscoll in action. I have." Sullivan harrumphed again. "You wouldn't stand a chance against him. Besides, I need him."

Scudder rubbed a callous in the palm of his gun hand. "You figure the Hubbard woman's still gonna try hauling freight up to the gold fields herself?"

Sullivan nodded. "If I'm any judge, she's got that Logan fellow backing her all the way."

Scudder rubbed his thin hand against his thigh. "She won't have him for long, if I could get a hold of a gun—"

"Shootin' ain't the only way to kill a man," Moose cut in heavily.

46 *L. W. Rogers*

Sullivan looked at the muscled, powerful man. "You got an idea, Moose?"

Moose grinned, showing broken teeth. "Man's found beaten to death, ain't no way of provin' it didn't happen in a fair fight."

Sullivan fingered his chin. "It's worth trying," he said slowly. "Where's Novak?"

"Makin' a round of the saloons, like usual."

"Get him."

They walked back through the night to the center of Fort Brooke.

Prowling the town, Logan found one of the biggest and rowdiest saloons in the red-light district and went in. He stayed at the crowded bar for a time, not drinking much, mostly looking and listening. With the probability of trail trouble from Sullivan's crew and the Creek and Cherokee Indians, he knew exactly the kind of men he needed.

By the time he left the saloon he'd found the first of them, Tully Hayes, a scrawny, seedy, sour-faced man in his late fifties. Although Hayes worked as the saloon's swamper, Logan found out the man had been a cow wrangler until he'd been reduced to his present occupation.

"What happened?"

Hayes lifted a spittoon from the floor and emptied its foul contents into a bucket. "Few years back, I was chasing a wild bull through the palmettos when my

The Twisted Trail 47

horse stepped in a gopher hole. I ended up with a busted leg that never healed right."

Logan figured if the man knew horses it was a sure bet he knew how to drive a four-up team; man who rode through palmettos could shoot well enough to kill rattlesnakes.

"Can you cook?"

The question seemed to puzzle Hayes. "You're mighty noisy, friend. Why you askin'?"

Logan explained about Denham and his plan to take the freight wagons north. "I'm in need of a cook for the trip.

Hayes went about his business of emptying spittoons. "I make a fair spoonbread 'n' fried sow belly, redeye gravy. If'n that's what you mean."

"I do. We got a woman on this trip. Don't know if she can palate your kind of camp cooking though."

"Reckon I can whup up a few footpies, if'n we can find some wild apples, and I kin take along a jug of sorghum for johnny cakes."

Eagerness glowed in Hayes's bloodshot eyes. "The way I figure it, cooking beats the hell out of swabbing spittoons and mopping up after drunks." The rest of his seamed, weather-ruined face remained sour. "What kind of pay you offerin'?"

When Logan told him, Hayes's sourness increased. "That ain't much for a man with all my experience. 'Specially when there's a snippy female along."

Logan told him about the bonus, though he was quite

48 *L. W. Rogers*

certain the old cow hunter would have been willing to work for next to nothing at any job less humiliating than his present one. He understood that Hayes's hesitation was merely pride-salving.

Hayes pretended to doubt as he considered the bonus offer. "Wouldn't get that unless we got to Dahlonega in one piece."

"We'll get there."

"Now, if you was to offer me enough of an advance. Been a long time between drunks for me."

The owner of the saloon appeared at Hayes's elbow, glaring. "What the hell're you loafing around the bar for, Hayes? You still ain't swept out the upstairs rooms."

Logan drew ten dollars from his pocket and put it on the bar in front of Hayes. The old cowboy studied the money briefly, glanced at his boss, then turned and yelled to the barkeep. "Redeye, Gus! Half bottle."

"Hold on!" the saloon owner snapped. "You know you ain't allowed to do any drinking 'til after you finished work."

Hayes sneered at him. "I *am* finished! I just quit. Got me another job."

Logan walked away, left the saloon, and went hunting for two more likely candidates—men dissatisfied with their current positions in life.

Shortly after he passed a wide, deep-shadowed alley a drunk lurched up the boardwalk toward him. A man of medium height, short legs, long torso, and heavy, sloping shoulders. A long white scar stretched between his upper lip and the base of his nose, like a moustache.

The Twisted Trail 49

He staggered head down toward Logan, who sidestepped closer to the mouth of the alley to avoid being run over by the drunk.

The scar-faced man appeared to trip over his own feet. He sagged into a low crouch as though to keep from falling on his face. Then, abruptly, he ceased to be a drunk. He swiveled around and launched himself straight at Logan. The top of his head rammed into Logan's gut and knocked him backward into the wide alley.

Staggered by the impact, Logan regained his balance, his feet spreading slightly apart and his hands closing into fists. The scar-faced man straightened from his crouch and came after him. A thick, heavy arm snaked around Logan's neck from behind and dragged him deeper into the alley. A fist came from somewhere to his left and bounced off the side of his head. The scar-faced man surged in with both fists coming up for a clubbing blow to Logan's face.

Logan brought his right leg up hard, the heel of his boot thudding into the chest of one of his assailants and slamming the man against the wall. He brought his foot back down and stomped on the foot of the man holding him from behind. At the same time he twisted his body, jammed his elbow into the man's midsection, grabbed one of his fingers and bent it backward until he heard the bone snap.

There was a yelp of pain, the thick finger wrenched from his grip, and Logan was freed. He twisted all the way around, striking out blindly. His fist sank deep into thick muscles and the man stumbled backward.

50   *L. W. Rogers*

Someone rammed all his weight low against the backs of Logan's legs. Logan hit the dirt facedown and rolled fast. He was coming up on one knee when he saw who the other two men were in the faint light filtering down into the alley from a second-story window. They were Sullivan's bodyguards—the hulking bruiser and the lean, surly kid.

It was then he realized they weren't just a bunch of yahoos trying to rout him for his money. He bellowed like an angry bull as he came up on his feet. All three of his assailants landed on him, their weight driving him back down, a hand clamping over his mouth to cut the yell short.

Logan sank his teeth into flesh and there followed a shrill yelp. The hand whipped away. Logan tried for another shout. A fist smashed into his mouth. Blood flowed back into his throat. He struggled against the weight of their bodies, his knee jamming into someone's crotch, his left hand closing on a throat. Fists pounded his body and face. Hands clutched at his arms, trying to pin him.

He managed to throw one man off, wrenched out of the grasp of another, fought his way up onto his knees. A boot kicked him in the temple. Logan sprawled on his back, consciousness ebbing for the moment.

The men grabbed his arms, one man on either side of him, pinning his arms to the ground. The hulking bruiser came down on Logan's stomach with both knees, knocking all the wind out of him. A fist like an anvil crashed

The Twisted Trail 51

down against Logan's head, triggering an explosion inside his brain.

"Hold him," the bruiser on top of Logan panted. "Hold him—"

He raised another big fist like a club and swung it full force at Logan's face. With the bruiser's weight pinning him down and the other two men holding his arms and tangling his legs with theirs, all Logan could do was twist his head away from the blow. He twisted it, but not far enough. Heavy knuckles caught him behind the ear. His head seemed to swell up like a balloon.

The fist went up again and came down.

And again.

Until darkness swallowed Logan.

Chapter Five

Matt Logan opened his eyes. Although the left one didn't open all the way he could see out of both of them. He gazed up at a heavy-timbered ceiling. After a time he raised his hand and felt the tender, puffy area around his left eye. He winced at the tenderness. Slowly he moved his fingertips downward and traced the length of a strip of plaster on his cheek and explored his nose. It was still in one piece. The fingertips went on to his mouth. His lips were swollen and torn. Some of his front teeth were loose, but none were missing. That surprised him. He let his hand fall back on the hard cot and wondered where he was.

Finally he rolled his head and looked to his right. There were iron bars running from floor to ceiling where a wall would have been. He guessed he was in the town

The Twisted Trail 53

jailhouse, in one of the two cells formed by the bars behind the office.

In the other cell a man paced back and for as though trying to work off some of his excess energy. He looked like he had a lot to work off. Logan guessed the man was at least a full head taller than himself, with a powerful, lanky build topped by the widest shoulders Logan had ever seen. Straight, black hair hung below the man's shoulders, and his face might have been stolen from an Apache statue carved out of dark granite.

For a while, Logan just lay there watching the giant Indian pace the confined limits of his cell. Gradually strength and feeling seeped back into him. With it came the awareness that his entire body hurt and he had a horrible headache.

The man in the other cell came to a halt at his locked door. His great hands seized the bars and, for a second, he seemed to be considering tearing them open. Instead, he shut his eyes, leaned his forehead against a bar, and stayed that way.

Logan turned his head toward the door to his own cell. It hung open. He tried to sit up, but found that his abdomen muscles were too sore to help. Rolling on one side he managed to get an arm under himself, eased his legs off the cot, and forced himself to a sitting position. Even though he got it done, it tore a groan from him.

The man in the next cell turned his face slightly and looked Logan's way. He raised his head and shouted

54 *L. W. Rogers*

through the bars. "Hey, marshal. Your guest just joined the living."

Logan noted the faint touch of an Indian accent.

The rear door of the office opened and Marshal Brody walked into Logan's cell. He regarded the man's battered condition. "How're you feeling?"

"How do I look?"

The marshal shrugged. "I've seen worse."

"Then I guess I've felt worse. It's just that I can't remember when."

Marshal Brody's smile flicked on and off. "Doctor looked you over. Couldn't find anything broken and, lucky for you, no permanent damage. I have to admit you ain't exactly pretty as you used to be."

Logan leaned back against the wall, exhausted by the effort of sitting. "How'd I get here?"

"Your friends carried you."

"Friends?"

"The three who were beating up on you."

Though Logan's eyes were dull, something in their depths smoldered. "Nice of them," he whispered.

"Not very. I was walking behind them all the way, with my hand on my gun."

"You always manage to be in the right place at the right time?"

Brody shrugged. "Sooner or later. Man passing by heard yelling in the alley. When he saw what was happening, he came running for me. I went over and called 'em off you. They said it was just a little fistfight.

The Twisted Trail 55

Somehow I didn't like the odds. Three of them and you unconscious."

Logan looked at the other cell. "Where're you holding them?"

"I'm not. Hell, if I locked somebody up every time a man took a beating in this town, I'd need ten more cells. If it'd happened in the respectable section of town I'd fine 'em for disturbing the peace, but . . ."

"Yeah . . . yeah," Logan cut in wearily. "I get the point. They say anything about why they jumped me?"

"According to them, friend of theirs was staggering drunk, bumped into you by accident and you played it tough, started to rough the feller up. So Moose and Novak jumped in to help him out."

"Their friend, he the one with the scar?"

"Uh-huh."

"What's his name?"

"Scudder."

"He wasn't drunk." Logan hugged his sore ribs.

"Moose, that's the big fellow, and Novak, they say Scudder was too drunk to defend himself against you. You can bring charges against 'em if you want. It's your word against theirs, and to tell you the truth—"

"Forget it." Logan shut his eyes against a wave of dizziness. Anger filtered through every inch of his aching body.

For a moment Brody thought Logan had lapsed into unconsciousness. When Logan did open his eyes, Brody saw the dazed, unfocused look. Logan's voice was thick

56 *L. W. Rogers*

with pain. "Keep watch on Clarissa Hubbard's room tonight, or you may have worse than a beating on your hands. Those three work for a man named Carl Sullivan. He tried to pressure her into selling her freight to him. She wouldn't, and she hired me as her wagon master."

"You saying that's why those three jumped you?"

"That's what I'm saying." Logan had to concentrate to form each word. "If you hadn't warned me about making charges without proof, I'd bring up the subject of Denham's murder too. So keep an eye on her."

The marshal scowled as he rubbed the stubble of whiskers on his chin. Finally he nodded. "Okay. I can spare a deputy for it. It's a quiet night . . . like most nights in Fort Brooke."

" 'preciate it," Logan mumbled. He closed his eyes as he felt himself slide down the wall. He was asleep when his head touched the hard mattress.

When Logan opened his eyes again, daylight streamed in through the small barred window of his cell. He felt slept out. Raising a hand to rub the last of sleepiness from his face, he winced at the tenderness around his left eye.

"Morning," a voice said.

Turning his head, he saw it was the giant Indian with the Apache face. He sat on the edge of the other bunk in Logan's cell. Puzzled, Logan raised up on one elbow and glanced across at the other cell. Both bunks there were occupied by sleeping men and three more were curled up on the stone floor.

The Twisted Trail   57

The Indian glanced over his shoulder. "Got too crowded in there. Two of 'em got caught breakin' into a general store. One's just a cowhand that got liquored up and made a pass at a respectable woman over in the residential section. The other two are his buddies who tried to stop the marshal from locking him up. Had to be pistol-whipped and carried in."

The Indian turned his expressionless dark face back to Logan. "Marshal moved me in here with you. Hope you don't mind. My name's Otulke Thlocco."

"That's a mouthful, friend."

"Yes. My white name is Joe Panther."

"You aren't from this neck of the woods. You Mexican or Apache?"

"I am Seminole of the Cow Creek Clan down Okeechobee way." At the Mexican part, he laughed. "You ain't the first to mistake me for a Mex. My mother was descended from the Spaniards. But I am a white man's wood's colt."

Logan looked toward his cell door. It was still open. "Seems like the marshal trusts you."

"I promised to stay put," Joe Panther said, as if that were explanation enough.

"What're you in for?"

Logan heard the regret in Joe Panther's voice. "Breaking up a saloon . . . and some arms and legs and noses." He offered an apologetic smile. "It's true what they say . . ."

When he didn't speak, Logan prompted, "What does who say?"

58 *L. W. Rogers*

"That Injuns and firewater don't mix. I was drunk, you see? Or I'd never done anything like that. The marshal can tell you this is true. He knows I'm no troublemaker. But I was drunk and some man made a disrespectful remark about my people."

It seemed Joe Panther was thinking back on the incident. "I don't remember who said it or what it was he said, to tell you the truth. But they say I threw him across the saloon and smashed him into the mirror hanging over the bar. Then it seems all these friends of his jumped me." He shook his head. "I did a lot of damage. What with the breakage and doctor's bills, my fine came to three hundred and twenty dollars. I'd spent all my money on liquor and couldn't pay, so I was sentenced to thirty-two days. One day for every ten dollars."

Logan studied the tall, broad-shouldered man. "You go on tears like that very often?"

"Last time I did anything like this was more'n two years ago. And I ain't likely to do it again." True to his name, he paced the length of the cell like a panther on the prowl. "I'm going crazy, shut up in here like this."

The rear door of the marshal's office opened. A deputy came into their cell carrying a pot of steaming coffee on a tray with cups and fat yeast rolls on it.

"Fresh rolls," he announced as he set the tray down beside Joe Panther. "Bakery round the corner just fished 'em out of the oven."

He grinned at Logan. "You look pretty fit for a man's just took a bad licking. My name's Jake Randall. I'm in

The Twisted Trail

charge around here for the marshal, daytimes. So anything you need—"

"All I need's some of that coffee." Logan reached for a cup.

"Don't we all." Deputy Randall poured three cups of the steaming, amber liquid.

One of the men in the other cell sat up and whined, "Hey, how about some of that over here?"

"Shut up and wait." Randall answered without looking around at the man. "Regular breakfast don't come in for another half hour."

Logan raised his cup to his lips. The coffee scalded going down. He gulped all of it greedily and refilled his cup before picking up one of the warm rolls. While he ate it and sipped his second cup, he studied Joe Panther.

"Ever handle mule teams, by any chance?"

The Indian nodded his head, swallowed the chunk of bread he chewed on. "And horses. I've been a scout, and I'm a blacksmith, but mostly I hunt."

"Best in town," Randall said. "Before you pulled the one-man riot." The deputy looked to Logan. "Took five of us to bring him down. He nearly tore my arm off doing it."

"I don't remember none of it," Joe Panther murmured. "You know I wouldn't do a thing like that sober."

"Done any doctoring?" Logan asked.

"Only Seminole medicine."

"Guess you're good with a rifle?"

Joe Panther shrugged a massive shoulder. "Like most everybody. Why?"

60 *L. W. Rogers*

"I'm running a string of freight wagons up to the gold mines in Dahlonega. We still need a couple drivers and guards. I could use a smithy with a little snakebite knowledge." Logan glanced at the deputy. "How many more days has he got to serve?"

The deputy did a quick mental calculation. "Fifteen."

"At ten dollars a day that means he still owes the town a hundred and fifty dollars, right?"

Jake Randall nodded.

Logan turned back to Joe Panther. "I might be able to persuade my boss to pay the rest of your fine for you—as an advance on wages. You interested?"

Joe Panther eyed Logan as though he were his long-lost father. "Interested? I'd crawl all the way to Dahlonega for a chance to get out of here."

"Gotta tell you. We're expecting trouble all along the way," Logan warned.

"What kind?"

"Snow, ice, red clay that turns to slush when the ice melts. We could get stuck in the mountains and freeze to death. Renegade Creeks, black Seminoles, still wanting revenge on the white man, and another outfit that's gonna try to stop us from reaching the gold fields in Nacoochee Valley, or at least to keep us from getting there first."

Logan touched a longer finger to the plaster stuck on his cheek. "They play rough."

"You don't know what rough is," Joe Panther rumbled, "until you been stuck in a little cell long as I have. Get me out of here and you've got a guard. And I *can* handle a rifle. Darn good."

The Twisted Trail 61

Jake Randall looked on the conversation, thoughtful. "Those guards you were saying you needed . . . what kinda wages you paying?"

Logan told him about the wages and bonus arrangement. "Why? You know somebody good that'd be interested?"

"Yeah." Jake's pug-nosed face creased into a smile. "Me."

Logan eyed the deputy over the rim of his cup. "Tired of being a lawman?"

"You might say so. This town life's beginning to bore me. Been a cowhand most of my life. Was 'til Brody talked me into signing on as his deputy. Sounded like action so I took it on. Anyhow he's got this town so tamed there's hardly any excitement anymore."

"You'll get more than you want with us," Logan told him. As far as he was concerned, any man good enough to work for Brody was good enough for him. Besides himself, Clarissa Hubbard had estimated that she could afford four extra men to act solely as guards. The old cow hunter, the Seminole, and Jake Randall made three.

"You're hired," he told Jake. "You know somebody that can handle a team and a rifle? Someone itching for action and open spaces?"

"I'll ask around."

Much to his consternation, when Logan met Clarissa Hubbard an hour later he found that she had already hired a fourth man.

Clarissa was stepping down off the porch of the hotel when Logan got there. This morning she wore a trail outfit: a split riding skirt, boots, sheepskin jacket, and a flat, wide-brimmed hat. It was quite a change from the satin evening dress she'd worn the night before. Didn't matter to Logan what she wore—she was still all woman.

Logan didn't much care for the looks of the man with her. He stood head and shoulders to Logan, was about the same age but slimmer, with long, delicate hands. There was a withdrawn, deadly quality to the man, something that emanated from almost womanish grace when he moved, to the contemptuous set of his thin mouth, the empty expression of his ferret thin face, and eyes like dirty ice.

Logan felt the man's gaze wash over him and returned the cold stare. The man smiled at Logan, but instead of softening those grey eyes, his smile deepened them to dark pits.

Intensified sensations churned through Logan and he hoped he hadn't met his future in this man.

Chapter Six

Clarissa's eyes widened with shock at Logan's face. "What happened to you?"

"Three of Sullivan's crew jumped me last night." He told her how the men attacked him the alley.

"Are you all right now? Will you still be able to—"

"I'm fine." His tone was flat as he looked at the man with her.

Clarissa introduced the two. "Matt Logan meet Reese Stone." The two men eyed each other and nodded slightly, neither man offering his hand.

"Reese and I know each other from before," Clarissa told Logan. "He kept order on one of the riverboat gambling salons down Mississippi way." She gave Stone an admiring look that seemed to Logan to be contrived for effort. "And he certainly did keep order. I've hired him."

"To do what?" Logan asked tonelessly.

64 *L. W. Rogers*

Stone's upper lip turned up into a sneering grin. His eyes remained empty. "To keep order," he said in a voice as deadpan as his face.

"As one of our guards," Clarissa added. "He can handle a gun better than any other man I ever saw."

Logan held down his irritation. "Has she told you I'm wagon master?" He met Stone's eyes, hooded like a rattler's. "That means you'll take orders from me."

"She told me," Stone drawled.

"Then I'm issuing the first order, take a walk. Miss Hubbard and I have things to talk over."

Stone's thin mouth grew thinner. He looked to Clarissa. She placed her hand on his arm. "You go ahead, Reese. I'll meet you at Denham's freight office at noon."

Stone's eyes slid back to Logan, held for a moment. Then he drifted away.

Clarissa turned to Logan. "You deliberately tried to provoke him. Why?"

"I've known his kind before," Logan said simply.

"Be careful, Matt." This was the first time she'd called him by his given name. "He's a dangerous man to toy with."

"And maybe too dangerous to depend on."

Clarissa shook her head. "He's exactly what we need. And don't worry, I can handle him." She smiled. "He had a yen for me back in Mississippi. I think he still does."

Logan's expression was as flat as his voice. "I thought you were going to let me hire the guards."

"Subject to my approval," she reminded him. "Any

The Twisted Trail 65

men you hire are bound to consider themselves *your* men. I want one along who'll be *my* man . . . all the way. Reese Stone fits that."

Logan's face softened. "I shouldn't have shown you so much of myself in that poker game last night. Now you don't trust me."

"I told you before—I don't trust *anybody* all the way." She put her hand on his arm exactly as she'd done with Stone and her eyes were warm on his. "It's nothing personal, Matt. Just a leftover of some unpleasant experiences in the past."

She was, Logan reflected, as used to gentling men as a mustanger was to gentling horses.

They walked together toward the freight office down by the railroad tracks. Clarissa asked, "Have you managed to find any other men for us?" She glanced at his bruised face. "Or weren't you in any shape to?"

Logan told her about the three men he'd turned up. She liked the sound of Jake Randall, but was leery about Tully Hayes and Joe Panther. "Hayes sounds too old and crippled for the kind of trip we're bound to have."

"Tully will stand up to it as well as any of us. He's one of those who toughen with age. And he's spent years dodging hostiles in swamps and open country. Just the kind of man we'll need. As far as Joe Panther, he's somebody who can keep an eye on what Sullivan's outfit is up to without being spotted."

"Where Tully is concerned, I'll take your word." Clarissa frowned up at Logan without flinching. "Not the Seminole."

66 *L. W. Rogers*

"I'm not much for explaining myself, Clarissa, but two things I know: men and horseflesh. You can take my word or not, we need Joe Panther. Enough said."

She crossed her arms over her chest. "Then you'll pay his wages." To further make her point, she added, "Enough said."

Although reluctant, Clarissa accepted Logan's choice of men.

Behind the small Sabal palm building that housed Denham's freight office stood a warehouse for freight storage, a fenced-in yard holding the wagons, and a corral in which the mules and horses were kept. Eleven men stood, waiting in the yard between the big Murphy wagons. Six were the teamsters who'd worked steadily for Denham in the past—rough, violent-looking men. Men who could be hard to handle on occasion, but would be just as hard to scare.

The other five had shown up hoping for a job.

Clarissa let Logan do the talking. He told all of them what they faced—holding nothing back—the kind of country they'd have to cross, the sheets of ice in the mountains that'd melt and turn red clay as slick as molasses on a July day, the likelihood of interferences from Sullivan's outfit and hostile Indians.

The six regulars heard him out with a stoic boredom, but one of the other five shrugged and walked away, looking sheepish.

Logan questioned the remaining four, rejected one because he'd never handled mule teams before, another

The Twisted Trail 67

because he appeared nervous and didn't ask about the pay. Logan had a hunch Sullivan had sent him.

If the two Logan hired—Banner and Carr—had reservations, they didn't show it. Both were big, solid men. Banner, ex-cavalry, and Carr had once ridden shotgun for the Butterfield stage before drifting to Florida. Both were well-acquainted with mules.

Logan went over the details of the wagons with the eight men. There were fifteen wagons, reminders of the time before Denham had gone bust, when he'd sometimes run as many as twenty in one train. Now some of the wagons were in need of repair. Logan selected eight that were in the best condition. Leaving the teamsters to prepare the wagons and select their mule teams, he returned to the office and gave Clarissa a $150 advance on Joe Panther's wages. Then he left to bail out the Seminole and collect Jake Randall and Tully Hayes.

He walked up the street where he met Reese Stone strolling toward the office.

They passed each other without speaking.

Marshal Brody made no fuss about losing his deputy. "Jake's been acting a bit itchy lately," he told Logan, "He'd've been sure to have got himself in trouble before long. And badge or no badge, I'da had to lock him up.

"He's young, pliable. You let him ride some of his wildness out of himself, Logan, and you'll have a pretty good man on your hands."

68 *L. W. Rogers*

And he was more than pleased to release Joe Panther, though sorry to lose the town's only good blacksmith.

Leaving the jail, Logan took ex-deputy Jake Randall and Joe Panther with him to hunt up the old cowhand. It took them almost an hour before they found Tully Hayes, sprawled out in a drunken sleep behind a stable at the other end of town.

It took another half hour and a thorough dunking in a dirty horse trough to get Hayes sober and on his feet. Even then he couldn't stand without leaning on Joe Panther. He surely looked old and feeble and useless. The way he was, Logan knew Clarissa would balk at taking him on. He needed him, maybe more than any of the rest of them. So there was only one thing left to do.

With Jake and Joe Panther supporting him, they got Hayes to the nearest saloon and bought him a double whiskey. Logan watched the old man gulp it, hanging onto the bar with his other hand. Drops of liquor trickled down his gray-whiskered chin. He swallowed most of the fiery liquid. His scrawny figure shuddered violently as it went down.

When the shuddering stopped, Tully straightened a bit and turned his bloodshot, red-rimmed eyes on Logan. "Another one of those," he croaked, "and I kin mebbe let go of this here bar."

Logan bought him another double. Hayes swallowed it like water, this time without a shudder. He set the empty glass on the bar, sighed weakly, and then turned loose his grip on the bar ledge. He straightened. "See?" he wiped a hand over his wrinkled face and, surprisingly, some of

The Twisted Trail   69

his years seemed to drop away from him. He even managed a one-sided grin. "Good as new."

"Are you going to need whiskey along the trail to keep you going?" Logan didn't try to keep the lead from his voice.

"Hell no. I only drink in towns. Never take any liquor along with me on the trail."

"That better be a fact. Because part of our freight will be a wagonload of liquor. I catch you breaking into any of it and I'll boot you out of the outfit without so much as a horse—no matter where we are at the time. Savvy?"

"I said I don't drink on the trail," Hayes snarled. "I just needed one big drink to kiss this lousy town good-bye, that's all. You don't believe me, then t'hell with you."

The strength of Hayes's anger reassured Logan some. The sounds of wagons took his attention away from the older man. Crossing the room, he looked out over the batwing doors at the street in time to see Carl Sullivan ride by wearing a rough trail outfit. From the way he sat on his horse, Logan guessed Sullivan was no city man and there was something formidable about him that hadn't shown the night before. Ruthlessness was written across his wide face.

The big bruiser, Moose, and the surly kid, Scudder, rode on either side of their boss. Behind them rattled Sullivan's empty wagons, drawn by their teams of mules, following Sullivan down toward the docks to wait for the ship. Since Denham's freight company sided the docks, there was no such need to get Clarissa

70 *L. W. Rogers*

Hubbard's wagons lined up for the arrival of the ship. A ramp led directly from the loading docks into the warehouse, up which the men could carry the supplies and roll the barrels of flour, sugar, and other food stuffs Clarissa had bought for Dahlonega, as they were loaded off from the freighter.

Logan counted Sullivan's wagons as they rolled past. Twelve wagons, each handled by a hardcase teamster. Riding behind the last wagon came the scar-faced man called Novak and four other men Logan pegged as gunmen.

Logan's eyes narrowed as he gazed after them. Behind him Jake Randall asked, in a quiet even tone, "That the outfit we're expecting to tangle with?"

"That's them," Logan said, half to himself. Sullivan's crew outnumbered his own by seven men. Bad odds. Maybe not as bad as he expected.

It might, he decided, be as good a time as any to find out what his own crew was made of.

Striding back to the bar, he purchased two full bottles of whiskey. Carrying a bottle in each hand, he headed for Denham's freight company, flanked by Jake, Hayes, and Joe Panther.

Some thirty minutes later, with the wagons ready and nothing left to do but wait for the ship, Logan gathered Clarissa and the men inside the one-room warehouse next to the freight ramp.

"I figure it's time for our last drink between here and Dahlonega," he told them, and looked at Clarissa. "If that's okay with you?"

The Twisted Trail 71

Clarissa made an open gesture with her graceful, slim-fingered hands. "You're running this game from here on in, Logan. I'm only the boss."

"Well, then—" Logan picked up one of the whiskey bottles and uncorked it. He handed it solemnly to Clarissa. "You first, boss."

She hesitated, until she saw the amused way in which he stood watching to see what she'd do. She glanced around the room, then raised the bottle, her warm smile taking in each man. "I propose a toast. Here's to Dahlonega, to a big profit for me and a big bonus for each of you . . . and to hell with Carl Sullivan."

She tipped the bottle to her lips and took a swallow. She even managed to do so without wincing. Logan admired her control.

Lowering the bottle, Clarissa passed it to her pet killer, Reese Stone, who hovered near her like a watchdog.

"I don't drink," Stone said quietly, and passed the bottle on to the next man.

No one else voiced a similar quirk. By the time the bottle had gone halfway around, it was empty. Logan uncorked the other bottle and tossed it to the next man in line. When it reached Tully Hayes, there were about three double shots left in the bottom.

Logan snagged the bottle out of Hayes's hands before it reached his lips. "You don't drink either, remember?" he informed Hayes and tilted the bottle to his own mouth, keeping it that way until he had swallowed the last drop.

72   *L. W. Rogers*

He lowered the bottle with a gasp, tossed it aside, and grinned at his crew. His eyes glittered with an excited wildness. "Let's go have a look at the opposition," he said and strolled out onto the loading ramp.

The others crowded out after him and looked at Sullivan's wagons and men lined up along the opposite side of the docks. Logan's eyes sought out Sullivan, held on him for a second, and then moved on to the hulking bruiser next to Sullivan.

"Howdy, Moose."

Moose scowled at him, puzzled by the lack of animosity in Logan's tone.

Logan started down the ramp toward him, his pace leisurely, his mouth smiling. His hands hung straight down at his sides, his long fingers flexing.

It wasn't Logan's hands that Moose looked at. He was studying the man's face, and as Logan reached the tracks, Moose's scowl become a sneer.

"What happened to you, Logan? You look kinda beat up."

"You should know," Logan said, and by the time he'd said it he was across the wooden planked dock. Without hesitation, without a word, without warning, he drove his right fist into Moose's stomach.

Chapter Seven

Moose stumbled backwards, clutching his middle, his face contorted as he fought for breath. Sullivan hastily got out of the way as his other bodyguard, Scudder, leaped at Logan with fists swinging.

Logan swiveled slightly at the hips, not shifting his feet, and backhanded Scudder across the face. The blow twisted Scudder's head around and flung him against a wagon. As he bounced off of it, Logan hit him with his other hand as hard as he could. Scudder's eyes went blank. He hit the dirt on his side and stayed that way.

It had given Moose a chance to catch his breath, though he still couldn't straighten up fully. Murder was written on his face as he lunged at Logan.

Logan turned to meet his rush, sensing the rest of Sullivan's bunch converging on them, hoping his own crew was moving in behind him.

He was in no mood for duking it out with the bigger man, but a wildness flamed inside him, demanding vengeance for what had happened in the dark alley the night before. He met Moose head-on, took a chest blow that threatened to break a rib, and smashed a left and a right hook to Moose's face with all the power of his shoulders and back.

Moose stumbled sideways and spat out the stump of a tooth. Logan went after him again and aimed his right fist at the big man's nose. Moose ducked. Logan's fist rammed into the man's forehead. It was like hitting a boulder. Logan's arm went numb all the way to his shoulder and for a second he thought his knuckles were broken. The punch didn't seem to affect Moose at all. He homed in for the kill.

Hard knuckles skidded off Logan's cheek, ripping away the plaster over the previous cut.

Blood pounded against the backs of Logan's eyes, blurring his vision. He felt himself crumbling under Moose's weight. A split-second later the weight was yanked from Logan's back.

He caught a blurred glimpse of the towering Joe Panther, his dark face a mask of fury, Moose struggling uselessly in the grip of the Seminole's enormous hands. Joe Panther raised the man high in the air and threw him headfirst against a wagon wheel. Then he turned, reached down for the man hanging on Logan's arm, and lifted him away as though he were a puppy.

By then the whole area had exploded into a free-for-

The Twisted Trail

all between the two wagon crews. A crush of battling men surrounded him.

A surge of adrenalin pumped through Logan. He staggered but stayed on his feet, bending forward and sucking air into his lungs. He took a moment to survey the action happening around him and to see where else he was needed.

It appeared that he wasn't needed anywhere. He'd wanted to find out what his crew was made of.

Now he knew.

Former deputy Jake Randall was getting up off an unconscious form when one of Sullivan's gunmen slugged him in the ear and knocked him back down. Jake's feet shot out and kicked the other man's ankles out from under him. The next second the two were fighting it out in the dirt.

Lame as he was, old Tully Hayes was engaged in teaching a man about twenty years younger than him a variety of vicious tricks he'd learned in other battles, including eye-gouging, nose-biting, and throat-kicking. Joe Panther was using one of Sullivan's men as a battering ram against three others.

And despite the odds, the regular teamsters from Denham's freight and the new recruits were holding their own against Sullivan's savage mass brawl. Logan filled his lungs, sucked in a deep breath, exhaled—satisfied at what the men were giving him.

Only four people held off from the fight, taking no part in it: Carl Sullivan, Clarissa Hubbard, Marshal

76   *L. W. Rogers*

Brody, and Reese Stone. Stone was where he usually was—at Clarissa's elbow, up on the ramp, showing no interest in the fracas.

At that moment Logan caught sight of one of his new teamsters going limp under two of Sullivan's men. Instead of letting up, they went on pounding at his unconscious form.

Logan reached them in three long, fast steps. With his next stride, not slowing his momentum, he grabbed one of Sullivan's men and threw him backwards. The man fell off the teamster with a thud. Logan turned to deal with the other one when the roar of shots froze him.

The shots froze everyone. Heads turned in the direction of the gunfire. Marshal Brody stood in the middle of the dock pointing his Colt at the sky. Several yards to either side of him stood two deputies, holding sawed-off shotguns.

With a slow deliberate movement, the marshal lowered his weapon, pointing it at everyone. "Fun's fun boys," he said without heat, "now you've all had yours and it's over. Next man who swings at anybody, I'll break his elbow or knee with a bullet."

Carl Sullivan took a step forward. "He's the one who started it." He stabbed a finger toward Logan. "For no reason. Just walked over and started pounding on Moose without warning."

Brody eyed Logan, who raised and lowered his shoulders in a slow shrug.

"Just a little fist fight, Marshal. Same as last night.

The Twisted Trail 77

Only this time nobody was holding my arms. Not for long, least ways."

Marshal Brody squinted at the crew of battered men. "I don't know what this is about and I don't care. But if there's any more trouble between these two outfits, no matter who starts it, I'm gonna hold all of you in town while I try to get to the root of it. I figure the questioning might delay your departure as much as a week."

He paused to let the threat sink in. "Okay, Logan, get your men back on your own side of the wharf."

Logan did so. Some of the men needed help, but they left a number of Sullivan's men still unconscious scattered around the dock.

Clarissa's stiff posture and the grim expression on her face left little question in Logan's mind that she was angry. She stood with hands braced on her shapely hips, waiting for him to stand in front of her. "Just what was the point of that, Matt Logan?" She spread one arm wide to indicate the group of battered men.

He wiped blood from his mouth. "Needed to make sure all of our crew are really on our side."

"That was a heck of a way to find out. The way some of them look, it'll take several days for them to be fit enough to do their jobs."

"If they can't, they don't belong in our crew," Logan said. He no longer looked at her. His eyes had strayed to Reese Stone. "Are you part of this outfit, Stone?"

Stone's hooded reptilian eyes stared at Logan without expression. "You know Clarissa hired me."

78   *L. W. Rogers*

"I didn't see you earning your wages."

Stone looked bored. "I'm paid for my guns, not my fists." He flexed the long tapered fingers on both hands. "My hands are delicate. If I broke a knuckle on somebody's jaw, I wouldn't be much use to Clarissa."

He had a point. Logan had known other gunfighters who'd pampered their hands like musicians. That didn't change anything. He figured his dislike for the gunman ran just as deep toward himself. He itched for a clash that would keep Stone from traveling with them.

Logan watched Stone move into a stance so fluid it was like watching a fine woman waltz across a dance floor. Stone's right hand arched slightly above his hip as he drew an invisible gun, pointed his finger at Logan.

"Bang," Stone said. Then he blew at his finger as if blowing away smoke from a barrel. "Sometime when the marshal doesn't have my Colts under lock and key . . ."

Logan understood the challenge. Though he was fast with his own gun, he knew he was no match for this shooter. Whatever might have happened between them at that point was pushed aside by the sound of a distant bellow from the ship's foghorns.

Two hours later Carl Sullivan headed out of Fort Brooke as soon as his wagons were loaded, pausing only long enough for his men to pick up their weapons from the marshal's office. Clarissa Hubbard paced the length of her office, impatient to strike out with her own crew.

Logan cooled her impatience. "We'll finish loading slow and careful, and get the doc to patch up any of our

The Twisted Trail 79

men who need it. Only a few hours to sunset. We'll camp just outside of town. Tomorrow morning's when we make our start. That's when we'll close distance between us and Sullivan."

"Distance? From what Henry Denham told me, there's only a few passable trails from here to Georgia. With a good head start, Sullivan can make it to Lake City and block our route, force us to backtrack, and . . ."

"Sure," he agreed amiably. "If he gets there first." He gave her a gentle smile. "But . . . he won't."

His certainty puzzled Clarissa. She wanted to argue with him, but something, something about the man himself that she couldn't put her finger on, stopped her. For the second time that day, she found herself reluctantly accepting his judgment over her own.

An hour before dusk, Clarissa Hubbard's wagon train rolled out of Fort Brooke. When they stopped at the jailhouse to collect their weapons, the marshal took Logan aside for a moment.

"It still ain't none of my business," Brody said, "but if you're interested in a piece of advice—"

"From you . . . any time."

"You need more men."

"I know. Problem is, we've got as many as Clarissa can afford to pay."

Brody scowled at him. "That's too bad. Because Sullivan hired a couple extras before he headed out. Neither of 'em exactly the mule-skinner type."

Logan nodded. "Well, I figured that to happen. Thanks for letting me know."

"It doesn't worry you any?"

"It does. But then, I worry about most everything. I feel more comfortable that way."

"Comfortable?"

"And safer. It's only the things you don't worry about that can hurt you when you're not looking."

He shook the marshal's hand and walked back out to the wagons. He untied his horse from the hitching post, set one foot in the stirrup, and swung easily into the saddle. He turned the horse to face the wagons, removed his battered work Stetson with his right hand, and lifted it above his head.

"Head 'em up, roll 'em out!"

Chapter Eight

They ate early and ate well. Tully Hayes proved to be as good a cook as he'd said. By the first faint rising of dawn Logan had Clarissa's wagon train on the move, proceeding northwest to rough country.

Hayes's chuck wagon, pulled by two teams of horses, moved out in the lead, followed by eight mule-drawn freight wagons. Like each of the teamsters, the old man kept a gun strapped to his hip, a rifle close at hand, and extra ammunition for both behind the seat.

Reese Stone and Jake Randall rode off to either side of the wagon train as flankers, one or the other occasionally dropping back past the last wagon for a look over the horizon behind them.

Clarissa Hubbard, riding a fleet-footed pinto with the grace of someone born to the saddle, acted as an extra flanker. She carried a Winchester in her saddle scabbard

82 *L. W. Rogers*

and a Colt .41 on her hip. Before many days had passed it was evident she was as equal to hard traveling as any of the men.

Joe Panther was gone before they set out that first day, riding off into the predawn darkness, leading an extra horse so he could alternate mounts for speed if necessary. No one saw much of him in the days that followed. Logan had given the Seminole the job of spying on Carl Sullivan's outfit. About every other night the Indian would reappear, have himself a hot meal, fill his canteen and food bag, report to Logan, and be gone again well before dawn.

Logan rode point, well in advance of the wagons, scouting the way. From time to time he'd ride a full circle around the wagon train, out of sight of it, scanning the distances through a pair of field glasses. He returned to the wagons only for the midday halts and when they made camp for the night. He chose and arranged each campsite with an eye to defense, corralling the horses and mules securely within a tight circle formed by the wagons, assigning guard duties so that there were always at least three out in the dark beyond the campfire light, watching and listening for the first signs of an attack.

Not that he was expecting trouble this early. To his way of thinking it did no harm to keep everyone in the habit of being set for trouble from the start. Because he'd been looking for them Logan soon found tracks, which indicated that riders from Sullivan's outfit were keeping tabs on Clarissa's wagon train, just as Joe Panther was on Sullivan's.

The Twisted Trail 83

The Seminole's first reports back were what Logan had anticipated. Sullivan was following a longer route across the flatter, grassier plains.

Logan had chosen a more direct, much shorter route— one that had a couple of problems. The first problem was a three-day stretch across country that was known for saw grass marshes with salt-tinged brackish water, peppered with quicksand. That meant conserving the freshwater in barrels strapped to the wagons. The second problem was a long west-to-east expanse of rolling sand dunes in which the legs of the mules and wheels of the wagons might become too deeply mired to get through.

They hit the five-day wet stretch out of Fort Brooke. In readiness for it, Logan made sure the large water kegs were double strapped on top of each wagon load. They stopped long enough to water the mules and horses to keep them from drinking the salty water. By the first night, the animals had drunk every last drop through the marshy expanse. Logan didn't appear concerned about it. He led the wagons an hour before dusk of the following day to what everyone thought would be a dry lake.

It was where there'd once been water, fed by some underground spring which had suddenly stopped flowing several years back.

But the lake was no longer dry. Logan knew he'd made a wise decision in trusting his instincts about Joe Panther. Only an Indian would know the mysteries of nature. As mysteriously as the underground spring had

84   *L. W. Rogers*

shut itself off, it had suddenly turned itself on again. The lake was half full of water.

Since leaving Fort Brooke, Clarissa had taken her evening meals with Logan. Their growing closeness appeared to irritate Reese Stone, who usually hovered nearby. That evening as Clarissa and Logan sat together after the mules and horses had been watered, she looked more cheerful than she had the night before.

"You knew the lake had refilled all along, Matt. Why didn't you say so?"

Logan smiled at her. "Wasn't sure myself. Had to trust Joe Panther."

"What would we have done if it was dry?"

"Gone two days without water. It would have been hard on the mules, but we'd have made it."

"And I suppose you've also known all along exactly what we're going to do about the sand dunes tomorrow?"

Logan nodded. "Passed along them when I was riding south, before the incident at the stage station where Denham was killed. It's windy this time of year, and the wind keeps shifting the dunes, sweeping some almost flat. We can bull through the higher ones, if we tackle it the right way."

"If we do," Clarissa said, "that'll mean we'll be out of the marshes and ahead of Sullivan."

"Uh-huh." Logan's forehead creased. He finished the coffee in his cup and held it out for more as Tully Hayes passed by with the coffeepot.

Clarissa frowned at Logan. "You sound very sure of

The Twisted Trail 85

it. How? We've been on the trail for over a week now and nothing has happened."

"For reasons," Logan said. "First of all we were still too near Fort Brooke for most of the week. Sullivan would want to wait until we're well beyond the reach of the law. He'd wait, too, in hopes we might break down without interference from him. And this country's too flat. You can see riders coming at you from a long way off. Besides, a man like Sullivan doesn't generally think much further than his bank account. I don't imagine he stopped to plan how he was going to get across Payne's Prairie."

"Won't he have a guide? Someone who knows places dry enough to cross?" Clarissa didn't want to doubt Logan's reasoning.

"Maybe, if he's got someone as good as Joe Panther."

"What then?"

"When Sullivan does get across the prairie and discovers he's behind us—that's when he'll do something about us." Logan set his cup next to him on the log. He watched Clarissa lean forward and stretch her hands toward the fire to garner its warmth. She was a woman who could tie a man's heart into a thousand knots. She had a smile that could roll back time, even if he was rarely the one she bestowed it on. When she was excited or nervous, she spoke in short, sharp volleys of speech, and, though she might be an opponent at the card table or in gambling salons on Mississippi riverboats, she could still blush like a girl if caught unprepared.

86 *L. W. Rogers*

He knew if he took her in his arms, her skin would feel as soft as wildflowers, her hair would run cool through the valleys of his fingers . . .

What the hell was he thinking? He snapped off the images flipping in his head. Having Clarissa along on this trip was a problem. A big problem. She roused him when he didn't want to be roused. Made him long for things he had no business longing for anymore.

"Logan?" Her soft throaty voice interrupted his thoughts. He shook himself from his musings.

"Yeah."

"Who is she?"

"She?" Logan wondered how the devil Clarissa guessed he was thinking about a woman. Not just any woman, but Clarissa Hubbard. "Ain't no *she* on my mind. Just trying to outthink Carl Sullivan's strategy once he crosses Payne's Prairie."

"You sound as if you know precisely when he'll do it and how. And exactly what we'll do to stop him."

Logan shook his head. "Not exactly. It'll depend on the time and place."

She stared at him in silence for a few seconds. "You know, Logan, you act like you can read every thought in Sullivan's head. And I've got a hunch you can."

Logan hunched his heavy shoulders and smiled. "If you want to play against a man, it only makes sense to put yourself in his place and figure out what you'd do if you were him. Everybody does that."

"You mean everybody *tries*. It's like that little poker

The Twisted Trail 87

session of ours. I was concentrating on tricking you, while you had already thought out what I was doing and what to do about it."

All this time, Reese Stone had sat quietly beside Clarissa. He tossed the last dregs of his coffee into the fire. Sparks sizzled and spat against the fire's heat. "Logan, I hope you turn out to be as good at fighting as you're supposed to be at thinking long thoughts."

Clarissa looked at Stone. "You've *seen* him fight."

"With his fists," Stone drawled. "Next time it'll have to be with guns. You've hired a fine bunch of brawlers, Clarissa. I'm just wondering how they'll stand up when the bullets start flying."

Jake Randall drifted over and stood listening to the conversation. He grinned down at Stone. "Don't fret yourself about that, gunfighter. We can all handle ourselves if and when the shoot'n starts."

Stone gazed up at him sardonically. "Can you? From what I heard, being a deputy in Fort Brooke didn't give a man much practice with a gun. There was always Marshal Brody to hide behind."

Jake's pug-nosed face flushed.

Logan said, quickly and softly, "Easy, Jake . . ."

The former deputy glanced down at Logan, controlled himself, and shifted his glance to Stone. "Be obliged to give you a demonstration." He pointed with his left hand to a small rock just near enough to be seen in the failing evening light. "Watch it."

His right hand blurred, whipping the Colt up out of

88 *L. W. Rogers*

his holster. It fired as it cleared leather. The rock jumped, breaking down the middle into two fragments.

He eyed Stone again. "Good enough?"

Stone shrugged a thin shoulder. "Not *too* bad. Sure it's the best you can do?" He stood up with a swift, uncoiling motion, his hands poised over the butts of the two revolvers strapped low to his thighs. "You looked a little slow to me. Try again."

Jake hesitated, then holstered his own weapon. "Okay." He spread his feet, eyes focusing on one of the two pieces of rock, his compact figure hunching for a fast draw. Then he made his move, faster than the last time.

Both of Stone's hands moved at the same time. His pistols seemed to spring into them. They roared simultaneously, before Jake's gun was even clear of its holster.

The two rock fragments smashed into bits.

Without bothering to look at Jake, Stone turned to Logan. "Maybe *you'd* care to give it a try?"

"What for?" Logan asked in a bored voice.

"I'd like to know just how good you are."

Logan showed his teeth in a kind of a smile. "Then we'd *both* know, wouldn't we?" He shook his head. "Nope. It's a waste of scarce ammunition."

The gunman's ferret face tightened. "If you're expecting trouble from Sullivan, some target practice for everybody wouldn't be a bad idea."

Logan stood up, dusting his hands on his thighs. "Anybody that needs target practice at this point, doesn't have enough time left to learn."

The Twisted Trail   89

He motioned to Jake and sauntered off to check the corralling of the horses and mules.

Clarissa rose to her feet beside Stone. "Logan isn't a man to toy with, Reese. Seems you two don't get along too well."

He turned on her. She saw the way his top lip twitched, heard the anger in his voice when he said, "And you and him seem to get along too darn well."

Amusement quirked her lips. "Jealous?"

His empty eyes fastened on her face. "You know how you acted with me back before we left Fort Brooke," he said tightly. "Not like that time down on the Delta in Mississippi when you wouldn't let me get near you. That's why I came along on this stupid job. And you know it."

Clarissa patted his cheek—almost a caress. "I know."

"If I thought you were just stringing me along for the use of my guns . . . making me wait for something that's not going to happen between us . . ."

She smiled at him. Her voice fairly cooed when she said, "We do go back a ways, that's for certain."

"Clarissa," he whispered, and somehow the way he said her name sounded exotic. He reached for her.

She raised her hand to stop him. "I think you've misunderstood, Reese. I hired you for your guns, nothing else."

The way he ran his finger down her arm made her skin jump. "Sure, baby," he said. "Strictly business, for appearance's sake."

90   *L. W. Rogers*

He held her gaze. His eyes were stormy, threatening.

An hour after dawn the next day the wagon train came to the sand-dune barrier stretching from horizon to horizon across their path. Logan was there waiting for them, having set out before dawn to hunt the best way across.

He stood next to his big buckskin horse between two dunes that rose like white waves more than six feet above his head, their crests rippling in the steadily moaning wind.

He'd pulled the brim of his hat down well over his eyes, narrowed to slits, and tied a bandana across the lower part of his face to keep the flying sand out of his nostrils and mouth. As the others neared the undulating dunes and felt the stinging lash of the wind-whipped grains of sand, they followed his example.

He gathered the men and stated the situation flatly. "There's no easy way across. So we'll try it where it's narrowest, which is right here. It's about a two-mile haul. Some spots have been blown almost clear. But there's longish stretches where it's pretty deep that'll take some doing. Let's get started by double-teaming the first four wagons."

Because the chuck wagon was much lighter than the freight wagons, he'd decided on testing the route across by taking it through first. While the teamsters unhitched the mule teams from the last four freight wagons and

The Twisted Trail 91

jointed them to the teams of the first four, the chuck wagon got rolling.

Jake Randall had taken over the driver's seat. Logan and the powerful Joe Panther went on foot, leading the first of the team horses and pulling them along when they hit the sand drifts between the dunes.

In a couple of places they got bogged down but were able to wrench the chuck wagon free. In one place the sand finally proved too soft and deep to get through, and they were forced to march out a detour where it was more solidly packed down underfoot. After a sweating, backbreaking effort they managed to get to the other side of the dunes.

With an hour lost, and the capacity-loaded freight wagons still to come, Logan knew it was going to be much slower going. Leaving Jake to guard the chuck wagon with instructions to give warning with his gun of any trouble approaching from that side, Logan and Joe Panther trudged back across the dunes.

They found the first four wagons ready to be hauled through by their doubled teams of mules. Because of the difficulty in crossing, Logan decided the best course was to take the wagons across one at a time. Assigning Reese Stone to stand guard with the waiting teams, he and Joe Panther guided the lead mules of the first wagon into the dunes. The teamsters from the other wagons followed on foot.

Halfway through, the mules and wagon wheels sank so deep in loose sand that they were brought to a dead

92 *L. W. Rogers*

halt. The teamsters grouped around the wagon, put their backs and shoulders to it, and began pushing. With them straining every ounce of strength, with Joe Panther and Logan pulling for all they were worth, and with the mule skinner spurring the teams to renewed efforts by the stinging snap of his long whip, the freight wagon budged forward again, balking against every gained inch.

At one point Logan noticed Clarissa had joined the grunting, heaving teamsters in pushing the wagon. He knew the little she added wouldn't accomplish much, but she was probably doing the right thing. It kept her too occupied to worry. And the sight of a woman pitting herself against the sand and the heavily resistant wagon drove the teamsters into using more muscle than they'd thought they had in them.

He expelled a long breath before he turned away. He had asked her to slow down. She'd answered with an obstinate smile. He admired her more than any woman he'd known since the death of his wife. Not that he'd given Clarissa any reason to suspect he had feelings for her. If he were honest, he couldn't even be sure she was physically attracted to him.

While he had read significance in every shortened breath she took, in the end it was Reese Stone she was playing. Logan rubbed weary hands around the back of his neck. No woman should look that good. The contours of her body outlined against her sweat-soaked blue shirt did little to ease his train of thoughts. What he needed was a soaking in a cold spring.

"Keep 'em moving!" he shouted at the teamsters.

The Twisted Trail 93

They kept the wagon moving. Every foot of the way was a mountain of toil. When they finally got to the other side where Jake Randall waited, the mules were trembling with exhaustion in their traces.

Logan immediately led the men back through the dunes, not allowing them time to find out just how tired they were.

They bulled the second double-teamed wagon through the way they had the first, then went back for the third. By the time they got the fourth wagon across, it was time for the midday meal.

The food and rest gave the men a chance to realize how worn out they were. Logan was relieved to find that he didn't have to force any of them to their feet when he called an end to the meal break.

By this time the mules that had hauled the first wagon had rested. They were unhitched and led back through the dunes to be hitched to the fifth wagon. This time it was even slower work getting the wagon across. But they got it done. Then the mule teams that had pulled the second wagon were used to haul the sixth.

Logan was both surprised and impressed to find Clarissa still with them, shoving against the wagon with the weary teamsters. And when they went to the seventh wagon she still didn't drop out. Although she was covered from head to toe with sand and looked exhausted enough to collapse, Logan didn't try to persuade her to call it quits. It was her cargo they were taking to Dahlonega. It was her money that would be lost if they didn't get there.

94   *L. W. Rogers*

It had taken an entire day to traverse just two miles. Now dusk closed around them as they got the last wagon across the dunes.

Logan had gambled the total time saved by taking the shorter route across the wetlands and the dunes would make up for it.

After making camp and tending to the horses and mules, it was a weary group who sat silent while they ate a quick supper and bedded down for the night.

With the sand dunes behind them, Clarissa Hubbard's group of teamsters traveled flat ground making good time. The wind grew steadily colder as October came to a close. Just as his name implied, Joe Panther had slipped away without notice to spy on Carl Sullivan's group. Now two days later, he caught up with Clarissa's wagon train with news that Logan had won his gamble.

Sullivan's outfit was more than half a day behind them.

Chapter Nine

The sun shone as a dull red blob sinking into the jagged horizon, casting long tortured shadows across a landscape that might have been created by the dropping from the sky of a God-sized jigsaw puzzle of stone and clay—a land of flat plains and twisting trails and towering massive oak trees. The wind wasn't strong, but its breath had become noticeably colder during the week's progress northward toward the Georgia mountains.

Logan sat his tall buckskin gelding atop a high flat rock, the collar of his sheepskin coat turned up to warm his ears as he gazed north to the rolling hills. He thought about the mountains along the Appalachian Trail, about how the snow gleamed on those mountains, tinged with a rosy hue by the setting sun. The clouds above the range were light and fluffy, containing the threat of snow. He hoped not yet.

96 *L. W. Rogers*

His saddle creaked under him as Logan turned slowly, taking one last survey of the other horizons. As he studied the south, he became very still. He raised his field glasses to his eyes, adjusted them to the distance, and watched dust rising behind the farthest rimrock. It might be Creek Indians, but he'd spent most of the day hunting for sign of their presence, without finding any. It wasn't Creeks he was expecting at this stage of the game.

Wind had blown away the dust. No more lingered in its place. No riders appeared over the rimrock. Logan waited, watching through the high-powered lenses. After five minutes, nothing further stirred where he watched. Finally he lowered the glasses, flicked the reins, and rode the buckskin down off the rock into a deep meandering gully.

The dry gully led Logan into a crisscrossing of shallow canyons. Something niggled at him. He hauled up on the reins and listened. *Reckon it's only the wind.*

He kicked his mount into motion again, cutting southwest. Half a mile farther on he found the wagon train filing past the bottom of a vast shale slide, with Clarissa and Reese Stone riding flank and Jake Randall trailing a quarter of a mile behind the last freight wagon.

Clarissa rode up to Logan as he approached. She looked tired from the long day's riding. At the sight of Logan, she straightened in her saddle, squared her shoulders, and grinned as they met.

"You're a little late tonight, Matt. I was beginning to worry."

The Twisted Trail   97

"About me?"

"You sound surprised. Are you supposed to be indestructible? Things *could* happen to you."

Logan nodded. "And have, too many times."

"Did you find a good place for us to camp for the night?"

"One that'll serve," he told her, and rode in ahead of the chuck wagon. Motioning Tully Hayes to follow, Logan angled northeast away from the shale slide.

Keeping pace with him, Clarissa said, "I've been studying the layout of the land for two days straight, ever since you told me Sullivan had somebody watching us. I haven't seen a sign of anybody."

"Don't get your hopes up, Clarissa. Whoever he is, he's out there."

Involuntarily, Clarissa glanced off to the left and right. She looked again at Logan's hard, impassive profile.

"Where?"

He shrugged. "Don't know, yet. I've made a point of not looking."

The wagons were halfway through a deep, wide copse of loblolly pines and a mixture of scrub brush when Hayes caught up with Logan and Clarissa.

"I like the looks of this place, Logan. Plenty of ways in or out. Situated just right to see anyone approaching from any direction. Makes it easy to defend, nice safe spot for camping."

"It is," Logan agreed. "'Cept it's not where we're camping."

98 *L. W. Rogers*

Dusk grew into night by the time all of the freight wagons emerged from the other end of the woods, cut to the right, and came to a marsh. The area was hemmed in on three sides by low hills. From the base of a limestone shelf a spring trickled into a shallow water hole.

Logan raised an arm to halt the wagons. "This is it."

Tully stared around. The doubt in his voice obvious, "Here? You usually know what you're doing, Logan. We're boxed in, no way out, 'cepting through possible quicksand. It's a death trap."

Logan gave the old cowboy turned cook and wagon wrangler a wolfish grin. "Looks that way, don't it?"

Not more than two hundred yards away, Driscoll had remained huddled in the dark shadows of a boulder watching Logan use field glasses to scan the area. Certain Logan had missed seeing him, Driscoll slipped back to where he'd left his horse hidden amongst a stand of scrub oaks. He led the horse until he reached the other side of the grove, well beyond hearing distance of Clarissa Hubbard's outfit. Mounting up, he rode south through the deepening night. He didn't push his horse too fast, rather letting the animal feel its way over the rough ground so that it wouldn't stumble and break a leg. There was plenty of time. There was the whole long night ahead in which to finish the job.

A little over an hour later he found the place where Sullivan waited with the rest of his crew and their horses.

The Twisted Trail 99

Driscoll swung down from his saddle to face Sullivan. "Either you're a mind reader," he told his boss, "or you're mighty damn lucky."

"Talk straight," Sullivan snapped.

"You couldn't have picked a better night for it. They're camped inside a little swampy area surrounded with woods. We won't even have to rush 'em. Just bottle them up in there, get our best spots, and wait for dawn. Come first light, the boys can start picking them off like shooting ducks in a barrel. Logan and his men will be caught with their britches down. They'll only have one way out, and if they get across the swamp, the rest of us'll be waiting there for them, nice and safe behind some rocks, to cut them down as they come out."

"Sounds easy," Sullivan said, half to himself.

"Just like a Sunday go to meetin' picnic."

"A little too easy."

Driscoll laughed without humor. "You'd like it better if it was harder?"

Sullivan nodded slowly. "Maybe. Logan's no fool. He got Clarissa Hubbard's wagons across the saw grass flats and the dunes ahead of us. He outwitted you at that stage station . . ."

"The hell he did," Driscoll growled. "I did what I went there to do, didn't I? And got away clean, with all Logan's poker winnings in the bargain. You should've seen his face when I . . ."

Sullivan was busy with his own thoughts. "If he knows you've been watching them all this time—"

100 *L. W. Rogers*

"Not a chance, boss. He didn't spot me once, didn't know I was around."

"You can guarantee that?"

Driscoll dug the toe of his boot into the dirt. He didn't try to hide the irritation in his voice. "You just heard me say so. It's not the first time I've had to trail somebody without being seen, you know."

Sullivan took his time answering. "All right. If you're sure. Take the men in. Get it done, and done right."

Perplexed, Driscoll regarded him. "How 'bout you?"

"I'll be here. Waiting."

Sullivan's answer surprised Driscoll. "How come? Never knew you to be scared to go into a fight before."

"And I'm not now. This time my only concern is getting my wagons to Dahlonega, and making sure mine are the only ones that get there before it snows. If I get myself shot down, there'll be no point to any of this." Sullivan poked a finger into Driscoll's chest. "*You're* the one's so sure this is going to be easy. And you're the one getting the bonus for stopping Clarissa Hubbard's wagons."

"And taking all the chances." Driscoll sneered out his answer. For a moment he and Sullivan locked stares. Driscoll backed down.

"Okay, *boss*. Just be ready to pay me that bonus to-morrow."

He turned from Sullivan to Moose, Scudder, and the others. "From the bruises I saw on some of you, I'd say Logan and his bunch had a lot of fun with you back in

The Twisted Trail   101

Fort Brooke. Tonight it'll be your turn to have all the fun. Let's go."

Joe Panther found Clarissa's wagon camp by the light of its cook fires. He rode in on a tired horse, leading another that looked equally weary, cursing a guard who demanded he identify himself as he emerged from the darkness. Logan strode to meet him, followed by Clarissa, Jake Randall, and Reese Stone.

The Seminole climbed down from his horse. He stretched as if to get the kinks out of his back. He looked beyond Logan at the marsh and the dark wall of trees. "Logan, you sure picked a helluva spot to receive visitors."

"They're coming?"

Joe Panther turned to loosen the cinch strap to his saddle. It appeared he spoke only to his horse. "They're comin', all right. Every last one of 'em, except the three Sullivan left behind with the wagons and mules. A lot more men than we've got. And right now they're all sittin' about an hour's ride from here. Waiting, I guess, for a fellow I spotted sneaking back down there apiece." He indicated with a tilt of his head as he lifted the saddle off the gelding and gave it a pat on the neck.

"Did he spot *you*?" Logan kept his voice low.

Joe Panther gave him an offended look for an answer.

"Matt," Clarissa voice quavered with anxiety. "Tully was right about this being a bad place to camp."

"He didn't say it was a bad place to camp," Logan told her. "He said it was a bad place to take an attack.

Don't fret yourself. This isn't where we're going to take it. Sullivan's men have got to come through that long passage out there to get here."

Joe Panther grinned at him. "Helluva place. I wondered what you were up to."

"Now you know. Get the men started pulling off that brush."

Jake Randall, who stood next to Logan, hurried off to attend to the bundles of dry brush and dead pine needles that Logan had set them to gathering and tying off with rawhide strips two nights back. He hailed one of the teamsters. "Let's get these bundles in the back of the wagons."

Logan turned back to Joe Panther. "Are Sullivan's wagons still half a day behind us?"

"Nope. Not no more. Less now. Sullivan's mules are fresher than ours. They didn't wear themselves down fightin' through those dunes like ours did. They're catchin' up on us. The rate Sullivan's closin' the distance, he'll be ahead of us again before we reach Dahlonega."

Reese Stone sauntered over. He gave Logan an amused grin. "It seems you ain't as smart as you seem to think you are."

Logan showed no sign of hearing the gunman. "Then the time's come," he told Joe Panther, "to slow Sullivan up some more. Get four fresh horses. Two for you, two for me. Take them all the way through the back side of the marsh. You being from Okeechobee makes you and swamps good friends."

The Twisted Trail 103

Joe Panther's white teeth showed in the dark as he flashed Logan a knowing smile.

Logan continued, "Once around Sullivan and his men, you'll be out of sight with them past the other end. And whatever happens stay there until I come for you. It may take a while."

Joe Panther rubbed his backside. "I'm getting a little saddle sore. You expectin' me to do more riding tonight?"

"Uh-huh."

"Hell fire, Logan, even Indians need sleep. Ain't had time for more'n a couple hours at a snatch ever since—"

Humor touched the corners of Logan's mouth. "Seems I recall you once saying how you could sleep with your eyes open. That's why I hired you. You can grab a nap while you're waiting for me, though it may get a little noisy for you before long."

"You sure expect a man to sweat blood for his pay," Joe Panther grumbled. It seemed the night had consumed him as he slipped off to pick out the four horses.

Logan's eyes settled on Reese Stone. "Speaking of pay," his voice stiff, "time's come to start earning yours."

Chapter Ten

Carl Sullivan's gunmen entered the dark piney forest riding two abreast—Driscoll and Scudder in the lead, followed by Moose and Novak with the rest of the men trailing behind, their guns ready. Small as it was, they made a formidable army, and Driscoll had already worked out how he would place each man.

The looming pines on either side of him shut out the starlight, making it so dark Driscoll couldn't see more than a few feet ahead, and all he could see then was more darkness. The moon shifted from behind darkened clouds, giving him a brief glimpse of boulders off to his left. He figured he knew the way. He'd been through this place twice during the daylight hours, and he prided himself on his keen sense of direction.

The narrow stretch was long. Driscoll and Scudder were still in it when the two men bringing up the rear

The Twisted Trail 105

rode into it. Driscoll's thoughts were already farther down toward the swamp.

"Driscoll—"

"I said no talking, Scudder. Voices carry at night." Driscoll's voice carried a threat. He turned his thoughts back to his plan. Halfway through they'd dismount, out of earshot of Clarissa Hubbard's camp, then go the rest of the way on foot. If they ran into any guards before getting into position, the main body of his men would rush the camp. Clarissa's group would be outnumbered as his men used the boulders and trees for cover.

He'd already picked his best marksmen, ready to shoot down every man and animal trying to break out of the trap. He figured this swamp was no different from others, and any who tried to escape through it would meet their maker in a quicksand bog. Quicksand—a slow, suffocating death. The thought pleased Driscoll.

Fifty yards to Driscoll's left, Logan rested on one knee behind a mass of rock, his carbine cradled in both hands, his finger across the trigger. He couldn't see the riders moving slowly past him, except as ghostly disturbances of the general darkness. He heard them plainly enough, the creak of their leather and the soft squish of horses' hooves on beds of pine needles. He held himself in, waiting.

His own men were scattered to his right and left behind trees and rocks. Jake Randall was the nearest to him on one side. Almost within touching distance, Reese Stone leaned against a tree, weapons drawn, ready.

It had taken some arguing to keep Clarissa from

106 *L. W. Rogers*

following them. She'd finally settled for joining the two men assigned to the other end of the swamp, to pick off any attackers that got through. Logan didn't intend for many to make it.

The pebble under his bent knee began to hurt. He didn't move. He continued to watch the vague movement through the darkness, listening, waiting tensely.

Driscoll felt the tension in his horse's bunched muscles. The animal blew and tossed its head, almost balking to slow its walking pace. Driscoll glanced quickly to his left, trying to peer through the wall of darkness. He saw nothing, not even the rocks and trees that rimmed the marsh.

He kneed his mount to keep it moving. Then Driscoll saw something dead ahead. Nothing he could identify or even be sure was really there. It was only that part of the darkness that—

He reined his horse to a stop. Beside him, Scudder wasn't so quick. His horse took two more steps forward, head-on into something that crackled and gave resistance. The barrier of ropes and dry brush stretched across the end of the swamp's entrance.

Scudder's horse whinnied in fright and reared back from the barrier. The two men Logan had posted there scratched matches on a rock. Each set fire to a cloth-wrapped stick soaked in kerosene and threw it.

Driscoll already had his revolver in his hand, hammer back, when matches touched kerosene. He fired at the flare of the nearest torch as it was thrown. He heard the yelp and knew he'd winged the man who'd thrown

The Twisted Trail 107

the flare. Both torch and man fell straight into the middle of the brush barrier.

In a split second the dry brush ignited, its flames licking skyward, outlining Driscoll and his mounted raiders.

Logan laid his carbine barrel across the top of the rock in front of him and fired at the nearest man revealed to him by the flames. The carbine stock recoiled into his shoulder. The bullet took the raider high on the side of his chest, knocking him out of his saddle. On either side of Logan the guns of his men rang out, the barrage thundering against the confines of the piney wood walls and slashing the raiding force apart.

Horses screamed in terror, rearing and snorting and unseating their riders. The orderly two-file line disintegrated into a churning mass of riderless horses, men on foot, and mounted riders fighting to control their frightened mounts, all tangling with each other in a desperate scramble to get away from the blaze that revealed them to the defenders' gunfire.

Now frequently hidden by milling horses, the raiders moved fast, becoming more difficult targets. Some of Clarissa's defenders fired at anything that moved, not caring if it was only men they hit.

With a gun in each hand, Reese Stone was one of those men. Earning his pay with a vengeance, he fired with neither malice nor regret. Each aim proved deadly.

In a flash of fire Logan caught sight of the melee below his position atop the rocks. He held himself tense for several long seconds. An acrid stench of gunpowder hung heavy over the scene.

108   *L. W. Rogers*

The raiders tried to shoot back but couldn't see what they were shooting at. Some of them didn't try. Instead they concentrated on getting out of the forest, back the way they'd come.

It was over in minutes. By the time the fast-burning brush consumed itself, the last of the raiders were gone—leaving behind only those who would never go anywhere again.

The abrupt cessation of gunfire was a shock. Logan drew a hand over his eyes, shook his head to clear it, and climbed down over the rocks. Using the lowering light of the last flickering flames he moved swiftly among the dead, twice pausing to use the toe of his boot to turn over a man who lay facedown.

He didn't find Carl Sullivan. He did find Moose and Scudder.

He stood for a moment longer staring at the scattered bodies while his own men crowded out from behind their hiding places to converge on him. His lips pressed in a tight bitter line and his heart thudded heavily in his chest. When he raised his head he wore a wooden expression, his eyes cold.

"What's our damage?" he demanded in a tired voice.

"One man winged in the left arm. One man dead," Joe Panther told him. "Banner."

"Too bad about Banner. He have any family?"

Joe Panther looked at him in the fading light. "None that I heard him talk about."

"You know what to do now?" Logan already knew the answer.

The Twisted Trail 109

"Yep."

Logan nodded, rolled the tenseness from his shoulders, and began ejecting the spent carbine shells.

Reese Stone sauntered up. "You think they'll come back for more?" His voice held little respect for the men he'd killed.

"No," Logan's own tone was dry. "Not tonight. Not here. They know our position's too strong for the number of them left. We got too many of Sullivan's defenders."

Logan looked about. He stood silent for a moment. "The odds are about even now."

While he reloaded the carbine, he turned to Jake Randall. "You're in charge until I get back, Jake. Keep a heavy guard here, so Sullivan's men can't trickle in and pull our own trap on us when you take the wagons out at dawn. And before you pull out have a look around, make sure they're not laying for you anywhere outside."

Logan's gut instinct told him there'd be no attack. He figured the surviving raiders would head back to their camp to lick their wounds. With the loss of so many horses, the men would double up, making their progress slow.

"When'll you be back?" Jake asked him.

"Sometime tomorrow. Don't wait for me anywhere along the trail. Just keep pushing north. I'll catch up."

Logan snapped the last load into the carbine, levered a cartridge into firing position, and slipped away into the darkness to meet Joe Panther.

Chapter Eleven

With each man riding first one of his horses and then the other, Logan and Joe Panther kept going at a fast, mile-consuming pace.

"How much further?" Logan asked Joe Panther.

"Should be there before dawn."

Darkness still filled the sky when they tethered the four horses half a mile away.

"Don't reckon Sullivan's men have made it back yet." Joe Panther stepped down from his tired mount and tied it to a tree.

"I figure as not. No need to take our rifles." He touched his holstered handgun.

They moved on through the starlit darkness on foot, Joe Panther leading the way deeper into a labyrinth of canyons and foothills.

Logan followed the Seminole down a gentle slope,

The Twisted Trail   111

reading with care so as not to displace any pieces of the loose shale. Both moved past a group of massive clay formations shaped like giant mushrooms, entered a twisting stone corridor with curved sides almost coming together over their heads. As they reached the end of it Joe Panther stopped, half turning to touch a hand to Logan's ear. Logan nodded that he understood. They were now within hearing distance of Carl Sullivan's camp.

From there both men walked Indian fashion, testing each step before putting full weight on it so as not to disturb any loose stones or snap a twig underfoot. In a low crouch they threaded their way in and out, keeping within the darkest shadows, crossing a stream of frigid water. Their boots making no sound at all, they went under a stone arch and through a narrow dry gully bottomed with rocks.

Reaching the base of a low slope, Joe Panther paused and made a downward motion with his hand against Logan's chest before starting up the slope on his hands and knees. Logan crawled after him. When the Seminole halted just below the slope, Logan moved up beside him and raised his head only enough to see over the rim.

Beyond the slope the ground leveled until it reached the looming side of an ledge. Between the ledge and the slope sat a scattering of boulders and Carl Sullivan's wagon camp.

Logan gave his full attention to the dark shapes of the freight wagons that formed into a rough square with all the mules corralled inside.

112   *L. W. Rogers*

The lack of campfires left nothing to see by but the starlight. Joe Panther made a vee with his two fingers, pointed to his eyes, then toward the camp to indicate he saw no sign of anyone left to stand guard.

Logan stayed where he was, his eyes scanning the night-shrouded wagons in search of any men. He was certain that Sullivan was too smart to order his guards stay near the wagons, with all those boulders around the outside of the camp. It was a possibility he didn't want to ignore.

Time pressed hard on Logan, urging him to hurry. He needed to get done with it and be gone before Sullivan and his raiders returned to cut off Logan and Joe Panther's escape. To hurry at the expense of caution would be committing suicide. Logan held himself in, forcing himself to take the time necessary. He had to know where at least one of the guards was before moving closer.

Logan remained still, waiting, watching. The coldness of the air and ground seeped through his pants and coat. He transferred his attention from the wagons to the boulders closest to the camp area. Time passed. His nerves stretched taut. Still he lay motionless against the top of the slope, studying the boulders with pinpointed concentration.

Then he saw something move in the deep shadow of a boulder off to the right of the wagon camp. Not a man. Not anything that could be identified. Just a movement.

He knew they were deep into Creek and Cherokee territory. This concerned him. Since the discovery of

The Twisted Trail 113

gold on Indian lands and the convergence of the white man, and now the rumor of rounding up the Cherokee and sending them to Oklahoma, it wasn't likely any of the bands would look favorably on this intrusion.

Joe Panther touched Logan's elbow. The movement hadn't escaped the Seminole's keen eye. Logan focused all his attention on the boulder. No one showed himself. The movement wasn't repeated. Yet he knew he'd seen it, and that it meant one of Sullivan's men guarded inside the camp. That was all Logan knew. He had no way of guessing if the man was sitting or standing or the direction in which he looked.

Logan sucked in a slow, deep breath and inched up over the rim of the slope on his belly. To his way of thinking any of the three guards might be looking in his direction. There wasn't much he could do about that. He tried to make himself as much a part of the ground as possible and to make as little noise as possible. Raising all his weight on just his elbows and toes, his head down and the rest of him barely off the ground, he snaked toward the nearest boulder.

Once in the protective shadow of the rock, he let his breath out slowly and lowered himself full-out on the ground for a second's rest. Joe Panther eased up beside him in the same fashion, his presence neither heard nor seen, merely felt.

Other boulders sat between Logan and the one under which he'd spotted the movement. Rocks large enough to hide a man. Logan studied the next boulder. He snaked-crawled his way toward it. Even though it was a short distance, the movement was strenuous and tiring. By the time he reached the next boulder he clenched his teeth to still the sounds of his hard breathing.

Resting, he spared moments for another glance around. Still the night's long shadows didn't reveal the location of the guards.

Only one more boulder lay between him and his objective. He stared at the deep shadow under it for long precious moments, goaded by the awareness that Sullivan and his men were getting closer with each one of those seconds. When he was as certain as he could be that no one was on his side of the boulder, Logan belly-crawled across the intervening space toward it.

Again he made it without anything happening. This time he didn't pause when he reached the protection of the large rock, but continued around it in the shadow of its base, making sure there was a guard leaned up against it on the other side.

The only thing to hide him now was the night. Suddenly the pale shine of the stars seemed overly bright.

He looked to where he thought he'd seen the movement. If there was a guard, either he was invisible or Logan's sight played games with him. The man might be standing or sitting or might be looking straight at Logan.

Logan slipped his fingers inside his left sleeve and drew the knife from its sheath. Holding it point forward, he inched toward the boulder on tiptoes, his body taut as a corkscrew.

This time he didn't move in a straight line, but angled off to his left so that the bulk of the boulder would

The Twisted Trail 115

no longer be directly behind the guard in its shadow. Halfway across the open space a brief burst of light from a match gave Logan the break he needed. Logan dropped to his belly.

The guard had lit a cigarette, giving Logan enough time to finally spot the vague shape of a man.

The man leaned a shoulder against the side of the boulder, a rifle in the crook of his arm. Logan tried to guess the size of the man. As he watched, the guard's head turned. Logan froze against the ground. The man looked his way, but not down toward the ground.

The instant the man's head had turned away Logan moved again, slowly closing the distance between them. The man unfolded his arms, dropped the rifle to his hand. Logan froze again, then resumed crawling on his elbows and belly when the man stretched, flexed his shoulders, and transferred his rifle to the crook of his other arm.

The guard scratched the side of his face, glanced off toward the slope up which Logan and Joe Panther had come, then looked past the wagons to the looming hillside.

By then Logan was almost under the man's feet. He came up off the ground like a rattler uncoiling for a strike. His left hand fastened on the guard's mouth to stifle any outcry. With an unexpected agility the huge man spun and threw a wild punch, landing a lucky blow that staggered Logan and drew blood from his lip. Another blow felt as if it had splintered his cheekbone.

For several minutes Logan dodged roundhouse swings

knowing the beefy man could easily beat him to a pulp. Then the man made the move Logan had been waiting for. The blade found its mark and sank deep and deadly. Logan held the man's sagging weight and lowered it silently to the ground. For a second he remained bent over the still body, his breath coming fast through his clenched teeth, his legs rubbery, his throat dry, and a bitter taste in his mouth.

He listened.

There was nothing to indicate the other two guards had been alerted, wherever they were.

Joe Panther appeared beside Logan like a shadow. There was no need for whispers or motions between them now. Each knew what to do next. Joe Panther held up one finger on his right hand. Logan nodded. Only one guard remained.

Joe Panther picked up the dead guard's rifle and held it ready. Logan left him and the protection of the boulder, lowering himself to the ground and snaking toward the wagons.

He was almost there when the report of a rifle somewhere off to his left broke the night's silence. A lead slug gouged a spurt of dirt from the ground six inches from his face. He sprang to his feet and sprinted the rest of the way in a low crouch, zigzagging as he ran. He hit the ropes stretched between two of the wagons. A rifle blasted at him again.

The bullet thudded into the wagon's tailboard next to Logan's shoulder. In the same instant Joe Panther fired, aiming at the guard's rifle flash.

The Twisted Trail 117

Logan watched the shadowy figure of a man detach itself from behind a wagon wheel. The man stumbled forward two steps, fighting to stay on his feet and bring his rifle around for a shot at the Seminole. Joe Panther fired again. The man pitched sideways and became a motionless shadow on the ground.

Another rifle crashed out from a rubble of rock piled high against the base of the mountain. The slug spattered against the boulder behind which Joe Panther had positioned himself. Logan had miscalculated. There were four guards.

Must be gettin' old, he mused to himself. Logan turned swiftly to his job, slashing his knife through one of the ropes stretched tight between the two wagons, then cutting the other rope.

He stepped in through the opening, entering the corral formed by all the wagons. The frightened mules squealed and raced around the enclosure. Logan smacked and elbowed the nearest ones to start them out through the opening he'd made. Then he ran to the next opening, slashed the ropes, and shooed the mules through there.

He climbed up on a wagon wheel so he wouldn't get trampled. He drew his Colt and fired it into the ground, showering dirt against the legs of the nervous milling animals, further terrifying them to more speed in their efforts to escape from the makeshift corral.

Two more rifle shots cracked from the rock rubble at the base of the mesa. This time they were fired at Logan. A large mule jumped across a non-existent barrier, knocking Logan off the wagon's wheel. Logan grunted

118　　　　　　　　*L. W. Rogers*

as he rolled under the wagon and out of the way of thundering hooves.

As the last of the mules stampeded out of the openings Logan had created, Joe Panther fired above the mules' heads to discourage any inclination of slowing down. The mules scattered as they ran and vanished from sight.

Logan left the wagon corral and sprinted behind the mules, joined as he reached the boulders by Joe Panther. The guard fired after them. Distance and darkness were against him. None of his shots came close to either Joe Panther or Logan.

Logan and Joe Panther spotted the mules ahead of them as they worked their way down the slope. Some were still running away, others were milling around. Several gunshots encouraged the milling ones to follow those that were racing away. The mules scattered in a number of different directions.

The first streaks of predawn grayness fingered the sky by the time Logan and Joe Panther rode away. They'd done what they'd come to do.

"Reckon it'll take Sullivan six ways to Sunday to round up those mules." Joe Panther chuckled.

"Never knew an Indian with a sense of humor." Logan slumped in his saddle. Bone weariness took over his body.

Joe Panther offered another grin. "Must be the white man in me."

"Yeah. By the time Sullivan's men get the mules rounded up and gathered in, he'll have animals too tired to haul wagons." Logan turned around and placed his

The Twisted Trail 119

right hand on his buckskin's rump, taking one last look as if to reassure himself that he'd done his job and that the remaining guard didn't follow them.

"By that time there'll be no way for his outfit to catch and pass Clarissa's freight wagons."

Logan watched his Seminole sidekick looking up toward the sky. He waited knowing Joe Panther would speak when ready. And then he did.

"Unless something happens to hold up Miss Hubbard's wagons."

"Is that white man's instinct talking?" An itch between Logan's shoulder blades told him it wasn't.

"No. Indian."

Chapter Twelve

It was a shade past noon when they caught up to Clarissa's wagon train. Logan said, "You're looking tuckered, Joe Panther."

The Seminole scrubbed a hand across his eyes. "If I don't get out of this saddle soon, I'm gonna fall out of it. I could sleep for a week. You ain't lookin' so good yourself, friend."

"Yep. I am feeling a might used up, and I ache in places I didn't know I had." Logan felt the tired quiver of the buckskin he rode.

In spite of being exchanged often, Logan knew all four horses were almost finished. He reached forward and patted his buckskin. "Reckon all you ponies have earned a good rubdown and some extra oats."

He spotted Clarissa riding the drag position on her sturdy pinto gelding. How beautiful she was. When she

The Twisted Trail 121

turned and looked over her shoulder, he felt as if she'd read his mind. She immediately wheeled her pony and raced back to meet them.

She was no longer the woman she'd been back in Fort Brooke or down on the Mississippi Delta, Logan reflected as she pulled up beside him. Her once neat and crisp riding clothes were sadly trail-worn and layers of dust covered her glamour. Wind and sun had darkened and roughened her hands and skin. A spray of freckles adorned the bridge of her nose. To his way of thinking she was still quite a hunk of woman.

A strange bond had formed between him and Clarissa. A bond of friendship and of something that went even deeper than friendship—something that had been forged during the many back-breaking miles when they hadn't completely trusted each other.

Yet the sight of her made him ache in places that had nothing to do with saddle weariness. He'd had a wife and a child once. More love than a man deserved in one lifetime. Then it was all snatched away by the Comanche. The lifeless bloody images still haunted his dreams.

"Matt . . . Joe Panther. I was worried." Clarissa's voice broke through Logan's thoughts.

In a flat, tired voice Logan told her what they'd done with Sullivan's mules. A chuckle escaped Clarissa's lips, then she checked herself and glanced back over her shoulder.

"Sullivan will want revenge for sure now." She didn't try to hide the skepticism in her voice. "How soon will he come?"

122 *L. W. Rogers*

"He'll want revenge, all right," Logan agreed. "When he'll come, I don't know. We've got about the same number of men now. Sullivan can't afford to lose men any more than we can. Both our outfits need most of the men left just to handle the wagons."

"Couple more days north," Joe Panther put in wearily, "and we can stop worrying about Sullivan givin' us trouble. He'll have to keep his men wherever his wagons are, to protect 'em. We're gettin' into Creek territory."

"Dang," Clarissa swore softly. "Now we have to worry about Indians too?"

"I warned you back in Fort Brooke," Logan reminded her.

She sighed. "Yes. You warned me."

"You didn't have to come . . . could've stayed behind."

Clarissa's soft mouth became stubborn, her dark eyes fierce. "I'm not afraid of your Indians. It's just that I don't have to *enjoy* the idea of a Creek attack, do I?"

Lines appeared at the sides of Logan's mouth and eyes. "Nope. Don't enjoy it much myself."

"What *I'd* enjoy," Joe Panther announced, without trying to hide the irritation in his voice, "is for right now to climb into one of them wagons and get some sleep." He glared at Logan. "And that's what I'm gonna do."

Logan nodded. "Can't say as I blame you, pard. Go on ahead."

"And just how long you gonna let me sleep before I gotta ride back to watch Sullivan's outfit some more?"

"Not for awhile," Logan told him, and looked away to the mountains looming ahead. "From now on we'll

The Twisted Trail 123

need you closer to the wagons. Like you said, we're getting into Creek territory."

Clarissa's teamsters moved the wagons through a long, mile-wide canyon. A couple hours before sunset a large group of riders rode into the end of the canyon behind them.

With five hours sleep under his belt, Logan felt himself again. He'd taken the position of drag, riding behind the wagons when he'd glanced back and spotted the riders' dust. He swung his horse around and reached for the field glasses that dangled around his neck.

As he focused the lenses, the oncoming riders slowed, bringing their mounts to a walk. Logan counted ten who rode in a straight line abreast, rifles in their hands. Sullivan rode well ahead of them, with a single man on either side of him. One of them was Novak.

Logan held his glasses on the other man with Sullivan for a moment, until he made out the red hair. It was Driscoll. And in his left hand, he carried a stick with a white cloth fluttering from it.

"Well, what d'you know," Logan murmured to himself. The pounding of hooves caused him to look over his shoulder and saw that Jake Randall, Reese Stone, and Clarissa had joined him.

"Sullivan?" Logan heard the tightness in Clarissa voice.

"Uh-huh. They're carrying a truce flag."

"Truce?" Jake stared down the canyon. "I don't believe it."

124 *L. W. Rogers*

"Neither do I," Reese Stone chimed in. "It's obviously a trick."

"Maybe." Logan wheeled his buckskin. "Let's form up and find out."

Within minutes he had the wagons circled up for defense, with Clarissa and most of the men barricaded behind the wagons or big rocks, rifles ready.

Sullivan held his hand up as a signal. His ten-man line of riflemen reined to halt. Sullivan continued to ride on with Driscoll and Novak. He stopped within range of his riflemen. And Logan's.

Logan rode out to meet him, flanked by Jake and Stone. He was sure that whatever Sullivan's eventual plans, the man wouldn't start anything here and now.

Halfway between the rifles the two enemy groups stopped. Logan knew the strategy was good. Whoever started anything now, all the men in the middle could count on going down first.

Driscoll grinned at Logan as the two three-man groups met. "Nice seein' you again, gambler. How're the cards treatin' ya?"

Logan looked at him wooden-faced. "I'm not playing much. Not 'til I get my money back from you."

"Figure to?" Driscoll's voice was insolent.

"Sure."

"Now?"

Logan merely cocked an eyebrow. "Huh-uh."

"Why not?"

"You're carrying a truce flag. Besides, it'll wait."

The Twisted Trail   125

Driscoll laughed. "It'll wait, all right. 'Til hell freezes over."

"Not that long." Logan offered a thin smile. "I'll get my money from you . . . if you're still alive when I come for you."

Driscoll stiffened in the saddle, losing his grin. "Any time, gambler, any time."

"Shut up," Sullivan growled at Driscoll. "We're not here to talk up more trouble between us."

In a quiet voice Logan said, "What are you here for?"

"I need more men," Sullivan told him. "I've come to hire some."

Logan smiled with his mouth. His eyes held Sullivan steady.

"It strikes you funny?" Sullivan said. "It shouldn't. I need more men and I'm willing to pay well to get them."

Logan looked at Driscoll's thin, surly face, then beyond to where Sullivan's ten riflemen sat their horses. His eyes returned to Sullivan. "Seems to me you've already got enough to get your wagons to Dahlonega for you."

Sullivan made an impatient gesture. "You know exactly what I'm after. And I want you especially. I'll pay you exactly three times whatever Clarissa Hubbard is paying you now to switch sides."

Logan said, "Reckon not."

"You made up your mind without thinking."

"Don't need to think on it," Logan told him in an irritated voice. "I chose sides back in Fort Brooke. You made it a permanent choice when you had your men jump me in that alley."

126   *L. W. Rogers*

"Never figured you as one to hold grudges. You'd hold a little thing like that against me when I'm—"

"I hold it against you." There was no mistaking the malice in Logan's voice.

Sullivan's cold eyes stared at him, saw that nothing would change Logan's mind. He looked at Jake and Stone. "What about the two of you? Triple pay."

Jake shook his head. "I'll stick with Logan."

Reese Stone said, "It's a real attractive offer. Unfortunately, Miss Hubbard happens to be a *close* friend of mine."

"Friendship doesn't cost anything," Sullivan countered. "Sure she'll still be a friend after you've finished being her lackey?"

"Be a little more careful how you talk," Stone warned. "Don't believe I care for the tone of your voice."

"All right, Sullivan. You've got your answer," Logan said. "You've made your offer, and we've turned you down. Ain't no traitors in Miss Hubbard's outfit."

Sullivan didn't budge. "If that's what's worrying you, any of the rest of your men who want to come over to me are more than welcome."

"At triple wages?"

Sullivan's smile held no humor. "Double wages. Teamsters aren't as valuable to me as men like you three."

Logan's smile was as cold as Sullivan's. "You must be worried."

"How so?"

"Ready to put all that money to buy men."

The Twisted Trail 127

"I'm gambling on more than making up for it once I get my goods through to the gold fields."

"Yeah. If your wagons happen to be the only ones to get there." Logan's smile deepened. "But they won't. You aren't even going to get there first. Because the answer to your offer is still no."

Sullivan looked past Logan toward the wagons. "Your teamsters haven't heard my offer yet. They may feel differently about it."

Sullivan's comment disturbed Logan. He knew Jake wasn't the kind of man who'd switch sides in the middle of a fight, and Stone had his own reasons for being loyal to Clarissa. And he was fairly certain he could count on Joe Panther and Tully Hayes's loyalty. The rest of the men was another matter. They were good enough men, but money was money. Double pay was bound to weigh heavier than loyalty with some of them, especially those with families.

Without teamsters Clarissa couldn't move her wagons any further. He knew Sullivan was banking on this.

"I'm answering for them." Keeping his tone flat, Logan said, "The answer is no."

Sullivan's lips thinned. "I'll hear the answer from *them*."

Logan tried to appear more relaxed than he felt. "Nope. And if you try shouting your offer, I'll put a bullet between your eyes before you get the second word out."

Driscoll's hand moved closer to his holster. "That'd buy you a hole in your gut, friend."

"Maybe. But your boss would be beyond getting any

128 *L. W. Rogers*

pleasure out of that. Besides"—he inclined his head at Reese Stone—"I've got a feller here that'd shoot your eyes out before you cleared leather."

Driscoll drawled, "Don't think so."

With his reptilian eyes pencil-point slits, Stone sneered, "You can find out, easy enough."

"Reckon you didn't notice, gun slick," Driscoll's voice turned nasty, "those men we got behind us. And you're in real easy rifle distance if—"

"You talk too much, Driscoll," Sullivan warned. "We're *all* too exposed out here."

"That's a pure fact," Logan agreed. "And none of us feel like bucking those odds against living. Do we?"

"You're the one," Sullivan pointed out, "that said you'd start shooting if I tried to contact your men."

Logan nodded. "That's what I said."

"Go ahead," Driscoll urged his boss. "He doesn't mean it. He doesn't have the nerve to risk it."

Sullivan studied Logan's expression and decided Logan meant every word he'd said.

Logan gave a slight tug on the reins and backed his horse even with Jake's and Stone's. "Time for you to turn around and head back, Sullivan. Now that we understand each other."

Sullivan stared at him a moment longer, then wheeled his mount and trotted away. Driscoll and Novak backed their horses off a few paces, then turned to join Sullivan.

Out of earshot from Logan and his men, Driscoll said, "Do we hit 'em?"

The Twisted Trail 129

Sullivan stared straight ahead, his face brooding. "No. We don't have enough men for an open attack."

"It'll be night soon, boss. We can sneak in and—"

"That's just what Logan will expect. Besides they're too ready for us now. As you learned the last time you tried it."

Driscoll's jaw clenched. "Then we've wasted a hell of a lot of time ridin' up here and back. This puts us two days behind 'em."

Sullivan didn't like the reminder. "It's my time, my money, Driscoll." His tone weighed heavy with nastiness. "And this hasn't been a waste of time. I'm this much closer to Dahlonega."

He stared at Driscoll. "I'll keep riding south with you until it gets dark, in case one of them is trailing us. Then I'll leave you. You're in charge of keeping the wagons moving until I get back."

He shifted his look. "I'll take your horse with me, Novak. You can ride double with Driscoll back to the wagons."

Driscoll frowned. "Where're you going?"

"Dahlonega. Using both horses, I can get there in three days. At the rate the wagons move, that'll still leave me plenty of time."

"For what?"

"Logan will be watching for us to hit them from the south. If they send a scout back to look, he'll see all of you sticking with my wagons. And he'll figure their worries are over. No one will expect me to hit them from the north. *That's* why I'm going to Dahlonega.

130   *L. W. Rogers*

I'm going to buy me some more men and bring them back down with me."

Driscoll scratched the side of his jaw. "You'll have to buy an awful lot of 'em."

"No," Sullivan harrumphed. "Not many. Not for what I've got in mind."

"Sullivan made an offer," Logan told Clarissa when he'd returned to the wagons. He was aware of the other men watching and listening. He looked only at Clarissa.

"He said he was still willing to buy your freight, with the wagons and mules. Fort Brooke prices."

Clarissa showed surprise. "*That's* what he wanted?"

"Uh-huh. I told him you wasn't interested. But if I'm wrong you can still—"

"You weren't wrong. Sullivan must be crazy to think I'd throw away my cards now that we've got a winner's hand."

"Not crazy. Just anxious."

"What will he do now?"

"Don't know. If he wants to try another attack, to-night's his best time for it. He can't keep riding his men back and forth between his wagons and ours. Every time he does, his freight will get left further behind."

"Then if he doesn't come tonight, are we free of him?"

Logan removed his hat and raked a hand through his hair. "I didn't say that. There's a number of other things he could do. It's the not knowing which he'll do that's worrisome."

"What do you suggest, Matt?"

The Twisted Trail   131

It wasn't his intention to cause Clarissa more worry than she needed, yet he knew she was a woman who didn't need coddling. "We stay on our guard all the way against Sullivan and the Creeks. We'll deal with trouble as it comes."

Logan chose their campsite for that night with special care. After the evening meal he had Hayes douse the cook fires and gave orders to the men that no camp fires were to be lit until dawn.

He assigned a full half of the men to guard duty among the rocks surrounding the wagon camp.

"I'll send a relief guard at midnight. That means everyone will have to do with only a half night's sleep."

One man from the group spoke up. "Fer how long?"

"Two nights at the most. It's the price we have to pay for security."

With the coming of darkness Logan saddled his buckskin and rode away to circle the area until Joe Panther relieved him at midnight.

Clarissa watched Logan ride out of camp. When he was gone, she carried her bedroll away from where the men bedded down, as she'd done every night as Logan had ordered. Out of sight of the men, she found a small hill that suited her. She concentrated on spreading the ground blanket and didn't see the figure of a man until he materialized in front of her.

She straightened quickly, her hand whipping to the pistol on her hip. She relaxed when she saw Reese Stone.

"Oh. It's you." She bent back to the task of spreading her bedroll. "You'd better go get your sleep. You'll be . . ."

"I don't need much sleep," Stone said, speaking just quietly enough so his voice couldn't carry to the men. "Never did."

Clarissa straightened. There was something in his voice that put her on guard. "Well, I do. So if you don't mind—"

His voice cut her off. "I thought you'd like to know what Sullivan was really after."

"But Matt said—"

"He lied." Stone moved closer to her. "Sullivan offered us three times what you're paying to go over to his side."

"Why didn't Matt say so?"

"I guess he didn't want your teamsters to hear about it. Sullivan offered twice the pay for any of them to switch sides."

Clarissa stood silent for a moment. "Matt was right not to say anything. Double the pay's a lot of money."

"Triple is even more."

She tried to make out his expression through the shadows. "Tempted?"

"Not by Sullivan," Stone told her in a gentle but mocking voice. "You know what I'm tempted by, Clarissa." He reached out and touched her with his open hand. "You feel like you look. Soft but . . ."

She jerked away. "Don't!" Her whisper was soft, but fierce.

The Twisted Trail 133

"Why not?" he probed. His voice equally as quiet. "Nobody can see us here. Why, back in Fort Brooke you led me to believe you feel about me like I do about you."

"I've led you to believe nothing."

He took her hand into his warm one. When she snatched it away he chuckled. She felt her heart pounding in her chest. A sound caught in her throat. It was meant to be a protest, but it came out as something else. A sigh, a moan, a sound misinterpreted by Stone.

He ran a finger down her collarbone and across to the top button of her shirt. He fingered it with his thumb and forefinger. "I'm an impatient man, Clarissa. I've got me a powerful urge."

His hands seized her shoulders, dragging her to him. She struggled in silence, twisting her face away. His fingers sank deeper into her shoulders, hurting. She went stiff and still.

"Let me go," she croaked.

His voice turned cold. "I'll have what you promised."

"I've promised you noth—"

His mouth bruised viciously against hers, forcing her lips open. Clarissa held herself stiffly, biting down hard on Stone's lip until she drew blood. She managed to loose an arm from his steel-like grip and reached down, grasped the butt of her pistol, and snatched it from its holster.

Something small and hard and round pressed against his flat stomach.

He let her go abruptly, stepped back. Clarissa gripped the pistol with both hands.

134   *L. W. Rogers*

"So that's how it is," Stone said in a flat, empty voice. He used the back of his sleeve to wipe blood from his lip.

"No one manhandles me." She struggled to steady the quiver in her voice. "I've had more of that than I can take. And I'll never let it happen again. Nobody touches me unless I let him know I want to be touched."

"And you don't want. At least not by me. That's what I had to find out, if you was stringing me along. Sullivan was right."

"Sullivan? I don't understand. What did he say?"

Reese Stone turned away without another word and vanished in the dark.

Clarissa knelt to the ground and slipped inside her bedroll. In spite of her bravado, she kept the pistol unholstered with her hand around its butt. Sleep didn't come easy. Eventually exhaustion took over.

She awoke at dawn, rolled her sleep gear into a tight bundle, and walked toward the chuck wagon. Tully Hayes handed her a cup of coffee. "Morning, ma'am. Coffee's good 'n hot."

The briskness of the morning caused Clarissa to shiver. She wrapped her hands around the cup to warm her hands. "Thanks, Tully."

"Boys done ate." Hayes served up a plate of fried fatback, grits topped with red-eye gravy, and hoecake. "Want a little sorghum to sweeten up the hoecake, ma'am?"

Clarissa offered the old cowboy a smile. "Just a little, Tully. Girl has to watch her figure."

"Yes, ma'am." Tully used the end of a spoon to pop

The Twisted Trail 135

the lid off a large can. He dipped in and drew out a spoonful of the thick brown cane syrup.

After she thanked him, Clarissa walked to the cook fire and sat down on a log. She glanced around half expecting to find Reese Stone gone. Over the rim of her coffee cup she spotted him leaned against a tree, staring at her.

She read nothing in his eyes and wondered what he was thinking.

Joe Panther rode into camp. He handed his horse over to one of the teamsters, then he strode to the chuck wagon. "I'm hungry as a bear, Tully. Hope you got some vittles left."

"I always save back a little fer you." Tully Hayes reached into a small burlap sack and withdrew a hunk of hoecake and some fried fatback. "Bread's a little dry. Meat's cold. Coffee's hot."

"It'll do." Joe Panther ate hungrily. He washed the scant meal down with coffee. "Logan make it back in?"

Tully used a wooden spoon to indicate the direction.

Joe Panther ambled to where Logan stood hitching a team of mules to a wagon. He respected Logan, valued the bond that had formed all these many months between them. With Logan, he felt like a man—neither white nor Seminole, but a man.

"I followed the trail of Sullivan and his men for a ways. They're gone—back south to Sullivan's wagons. All 'cept one who took off with a spare horse, circled past us to the east over there." Joe Panther indicated with his head.

136 *L. W. Rogers*

"Reckon Sullivan wants him to keep an eye on us, like before." Logan's nod held no special meaning to it. "Could be he's calling it quits."

Joe Panther chewed thoughtfully on the last of the hoecake. He washed the fried bread down with coffee. "Could be, but when my scalp itches the Indian part of me says something ain't right."

"And?"

"I'd agree that Sullivan is calling it quits, if it wasn't for him sending a man to keep track of us again."

Logan said, "Yeah. Sullivan hasn't quit." He looked up at the sky and how the big clouds had formed over the mountains during the night.

"What's your Indian itch say about the weather?"

Joe Panther grinned. "Gonna snow." He bunched his jacket closer around his neck. "Sure do miss all that Florida sunshine."

"And swattin' mosquitoes?" The jest from Logan required no answer. "Snow or Sullivan. Neither are good odds." Logan rechecked the wagon traces. "It'll take us ten more days to get to Dahlonega. More if those snow clouds decide to open up."

"Yeah. And a lot of time for something to happen in." Joe Panther ambled toward the chuck wagon and sat his cup on the tailback. He caught sight of Reese Stone as he walked over to where the horses stood tethered. He didn't need his Seminole's sixth sense to tell him the gun slick was trouble.

Chapter Thirteen

Later that night Tully Hayes scooped hot embers from the cook fire into an iron Dutch-oven and set the lid in place. He carried it to the rear of the wagon where Clarissa stood.

"Beg pardon, ma'am. This ain't nothing like one of them fancy coal do-dahs that keep ladies warm on a cold night." He handed Clarissa the pot. "I got to allow how Joe Panther is right 'bout the shift in weather. You set this inside your blanket, down at the end. If'n your feet are warm, you'll be warm all over." He shifted on his feet. "Meaning no disrespect, ma'am."

He had come as close to being a father figure as Clarissa had ever known. She liked the way he fussed over her without being obtrusive.

"None taken." She shifted her bedroll to under her arm. She needed both hands to carry the heavy

138 *L. W. Rogers*

vessel. "Mighty thoughtful of you, Tully. You stay warm too."

She refrained from kissing the old man on his cheek, knowing it would breech ethics.

The next morning as Clarissa's freight wagons moved out, small flurries of snow swirled like cotton floating on air. By their second night snow began to fall in the mountains. Before noon the mules struggled to haul the heavy wagons up between thickly forested slopes.

Tangles of dead trees and branches that had tumbled down the slope and the snowfall made the trail difficult.

After an hour the snow stopped and Clarissa's wagon train continued slowly upward, aiming at a pass that showed only as a distant notch between the two jagged peaks rising above the timberline. Late that afternoon another snow flurry hit.

Logan squinted upward. Though the flurry had lasted only an hour, he knew this was only a prelude. The clouds had merged during the day into one solid overhang that completely blotted out the sky.

Temperatures dropped again during the night, and snow fell steadily for a couple of hours. At dawn, the wagons and the land around them lay in a blanket of white.

Logan watched Jake Randall trudge toward him. He grinned at the former deputy. "Guess you're missing Florida."

Jake blew at his fisted hands. His warm breath steamed in the cold. "Yeah, what I wouldn't give for

The Twisted Trail 139

some hot sunshine right about now." He, too, watched the sky. "Reckon there'll be more snow? The mules will have a hard time pulling the wagons."

"Before he left camp, Joe Panther said he could taste it and smell it in the air." Logan hunched his shoulders against the cold. "I trust his instincts."

Jake stamped his feet as if trying to put circulation back into them. "One consolation, though."

"Yeah? What's that?"

Logan thought he noticed a mischievous twinkle in Jake's eyes. "Sullivan is behind us, right? He'll have to follow in our wagon ruts. Catch my drift?"

"I like the way you think, Jake. Snow made even wetter when our wagons pull through it will make deep, slick ruts. Sullivan's going to have a tougher going than us."

Logan glanced over at the teamsters. The haggard looks on their faces told him that the past nights of getting only half their sleep had taken a toll on them.

"Gather 'round men," he announced. "You'll go back to alternating three-men watches tonight."

He knew this was risky, but necessary. Sleep deprived, worn-out men couldn't handle mule teams over rugged terrain or be fully ready when trouble came.

The men grumbled. One man spoke up. "Ain't right. Pushin' men like they was animals."

Logan wanted to tell the man he could draw his pay and leave. One rabble-rouser could stir the entire group to quit, and Logan needed every last man. "You knew the odds when you signed on."

140 *L. W. Rogers*

A staring match took place between Logan and the teamster. The teamster backed down, but not without a last word. "Hope the bonus the lady pays us is worth it."

Joe Panther returned in time for breakfast from an absence of a day and night, with news that Sullivan's train was also in the mountains.

"They're following another trail," he told Logan while he ate. "Over that way." He nodded eastward. "Good as this one and shorter."

Logan nodded, looking to the east. "Good as this one?"

"Shorter. I scouted it. Farther on there're some long, narrow ledges they'll have to travel over that'll get blocked up if it snows steady for a couple of days. Not worth the risk." The Seminole swallowed a mouthful of coffee, blinked as the heat of it brought tears to is eyes.

"They're comin' along at a good pace so far. Might be another day and a half before they get as far north as we are right now."

Logan turned to him. "See any Creek sign?"

"Uh-huh. But old sign. How 'bout you?"

"Same thing. Indian pony tracks, made about a week ago."

Joe Panther glanced reflectively at the surrounding peaks and ridges. "Means they ain't close. Also means they're around us somewhere."

"Sure would like to know exactly where. By the way, what took you so long? Expected you back last night."

The Twisted Trail 141

"I decided to do my sleepin' on the trail." Joe Panther heaved a sigh, followed by a grin. "You usually got more work for me soon's I show up."

"Seems so," Logan admitted. He dusted snow from his trousers. "After you finish filling your belly, you can ride flank over to your left."

Logan liked the Seminole and trusted him more than he'd trusted most men. Logan thought about the irony of it—seeing how it was Indians who'd killed his family while he was scouting for the Army up Arizona way.

He assigned Jake Randall to the right flank. Stone to ride drag. He left to check on Clarissa.

"Ride in the wagon with Tully."

He raised his hand to stop her protest. "Trails are narrow and slippery. If you value your pinto as much as I think you do, you'll spare the animal. One misstep and you'll both be over the mountain."

"Could happen just as well in the wagon."

"Your choice, Clarissa. Stubbornness or good sense."

He didn't wait for her answer. Instead he wheeled his buckskin and rode away from the camp.

The wagons entered the pass after the midday meal. Logan had ridden out to do an advance scout when snow began falling again. At the same time he spotted the tracks of an unshod pony crossing his path.

The tracks led to the east, and unlike others he'd spotted these were fresh tracks, their imprints sharp in the frosted slush and beginning to fill up with the new snow.

142   *L. W. Rogers*

He leaned forward in his saddle, his narrowed eyes following the hoof marks where they vanished behind the curtain of snowflakes. With the slightest movement, he drew the carbine from its scabbard, reined his buckskin to the right, and followed the tracks.

He rode tensed, knowing his prey might also be hunting him. Fat, soft flakes came down steadily in the windless air obscuring Logan's visibility, increasing the danger of being ambushed. He didn't like how the weather forced him to slow his pace. The crunch of snow under his horse's hooves sounded louder against the silent woods. Snow rapidly filled the unshod pony's hoof marks. Logan leaned over Buck's shoulder so as not lose sight of trail.

After a half an hour, the tracks cut south, then finally disappeared, blanketed under the fresh snow. Logan pulled up. His horse pawed at the snow.

"Easy, Buck. We're both cold." Logan scanned the white world around him. Then he rode on through the maze of snow-shrouded boulders and pines, circling behind the wagon train and up the other side of it. He came across no further sign of the Indian.

Logan topped a small rise. He caught sight of the wagon trail to the west and rode down to meet it.

Joe Panther rode flank. Logan pulled his buckskin alongside the Seminole's sorrel. "I just crossed the tracks of an Indian pony." Logan's voice held little expression. "Nice fresh ones this time."

He noticed this information seemed to have little ef-

The Twisted Trail   143

fect on the Seminole. Joe Panther said, "You were wondering where they were. Now you know."

"No," Logan said, "only know *one* is too close for comfort."

Joe Panther looked at him. "Never knew a Creek or a Cherokee to travel alone—not for long. You're a bettin' man. I'll give you odds there's more where he came from, not more'n five hours ride from here."

Logan eyed Joe Panther. "I don't bet against a pat hand."

"He'll just have himself a good look at us, make sure how many guns we got before hightailin' it off to his war party with the good news. Then they'll all be payin' us a visit."

"Maybe. Depends how many guns *they've* got." Logan looked across to where the wagons moved eastward. Jake Randall was supposed to be riding the other flank. He wasn't there. In spite of the falling snow he should have been close enough to be seen.

"Where's Jake?" The tightness in Logan's voice was unmistakable.

Joe Panther looked off in the same direction and scowled. "Dunno. He was over there last time I looked."

"Exactly where'd you see him last?"

"Back there by that break in the rocks." Joe Panther didn't point. "Maybe Jake saw somethin' in there and went for a closer look."

"Yeah, that's what I'm afraid of. I'll go look for him."

"Maybe I better come with you."

144   *L. W. Rogers*

"No. Stick with the wagons. If I'm not back by dark, pick a safe campsite."

"And if you don't come back ever?"

"I'll be back," Logan told him as he turned his buckskin away. "Only the good die young."

"You're gettin' older by the minute," Joe Panther said, but Logan was already out of earshot.

He didn't ride directly to the east. Instead he went west until Joe Panther was swallowed up behind him by the falling snow. Then he turned south and rode a long circle behind the wagons. He cut north again. By the time he was well east of the wagon train, it was beyond his sight.

When he came to a narrow pass through the rocks where Joe Panther had last seen Jake, Logan halted his horse and dismounted. He tethered the buckskin inside a thick stand of high spruce and removed his carbine from its scabbard. He continued on foot. Moving at a crouch that gave him the protection of the rocks and bushes along the way, he came in sight of a charred pine truck. He squatted behind a clump of gooseberry bushes and scanned the bottom of the gorge that cut east from the pass.

If Jake Randall had turned away from the wagon trail there, his tracks had been smothered under the falling snow.

Logan remained where he was for a time, considering the possibilities and not liking any of them. Then he moved on, keeping just below a humped line of ridge, following the direction of the pass. He kept his finger

The Twisted Trail

against the carbine's trigger guard. Every twenty yards he paused to scrutinize all possible cover within sight. The pass widened and grew deeper, then opened into a cross-cut ravine through which a shallow rock-choked stream rushed down through the mountains. Logan eased himself into a cluster of snow-covered rocks for a look into the ravine below.

He didn't like what he saw.

Jake Randall lay face down in the stream, the back of his head and body showing above the white foam of water. His arms and legs were sprawled out from him, toes touching the near bank, hands almost reaching the other bank.

A heavy knot formed in the pit of Logan's stomach. His eyes dulled. The lines of his face became slack, then slowly hardened again.

He bellied down in the snow and stayed that way, very still. Jake was dead and nothing could be done for him. To go down to his body now would be pointless and possible suicide.

Jake's horse wasn't in the ravine. Logan studied the dense thicket of pine, spruce, and balsam on the other side of the stream. The Creek might have taken Jake's horse and be on his way by now. Logan didn't think so. He figured the Creek might wait within sight of the body—long enough to see if anybody came looking for Jake.

If a single man came searching, the Indian would wait until the man got to Jake's body. Then there would be two bodies in the stream and two horses to take away as pickings—something for a warrior to boast of for the rest of his life.

If more than one man came, a Creek could easily slip away in the thick forest on the other side of the stream.

Logan stayed where he was, hidden among the rocks, not moving though the intense cold began to numb the flesh of his face and hands. He scanned the thicket opposite for any unnatural line of shadow, any snow dropping from a shaken bough. He saw nothing unnatural; nothing moved. He lay patient. Snow began to cover him, merging his form with the general whiteness all around.

The limit of the time the Indian would wait was reached and passed. Logan knew the wagon train was moving farther away. If anyone was going to come looking for Jake, he should have come by now. It was time for the Creek to relinquish his ambush position and take word of the wagon train to his bunch.

Logan continued to wait, gambling that someone was there on the other side of the stream, and that he wouldn't leave by merely fading deeper into the forest. There were easier ways, he knew, for a man on horseback to get out of the ravine.

He decided to give himself ten more minutes of waiting. It paid off. A dense tangle of balsam on the other side of the stream betrayed movement.

A Creek warrior emerged astride a spotted pony, leading Jake's horse and carrying a rifle in one hand. He paused for a glance at Jake's body in the stream and a swift survey of the surrounding area. His searching

The Twisted Trail 147

glance moved directly over the rocks where Logan lay. Logan's breath caught in his throat. He didn't want to alert the Indian.

Logan could have shot him then. He wanted to. Wanted to avenge Jake. But the need to find out the location and size of the band the Creek belonged to was more important. He waited until the Indian turned his pony and started up the ravine along the stream bank. Then he squirmed backward out of the rocks and rushed to his own horse. Mounting up, he rode into the pass. Reaching the ravine, he crossed he stream without looking at Jake's corpse.

When he reached the other side, he found that the snowfall had already obscured the trail left by the Indian pony and Jake's horse. Logan kneed the buckskin, urging him to a faster pace, squinting ahead to make sure he didn't approach within sight of his prey. When the tracks became more distinct he slowed his horse a bit, but not too much.

Trailing a Creek warrior this close was dangerous. Indians had a habit of watching their back trail, and they learned ambush technique before they could walk. At the rate the snow fell, to drop back farther would be to risk losing the tracks entirely. Logan kept the distance between himself and the Indian to what it was. He kept the carbine ready in his hand, his finger close to the trigger.

The Creek's trail led out the north end of the ravine and cut east with the stream. It entered an expanding gorge with rising walls along which stunted scrub pine

148 *L. W. Rogers*

sank roots among great outcroppings of rock. Logan followed the tracks for over an hour. Then they turned north, still following the stream.

The stream angled and twisted, now east, then back north again. Following the tracks beside it, Logan caught sight of a pass farther east of him—the pass where Sullivan's wagons would be coming.

Dusk came early because of the overcast sky. About the same time the falling snowflakes lessened. It continued to snow, but less thickly. This meant the tracks Logan followed filled up more slowly. He could see farther ahead, and at the same time drop farther behind the Indian without losing his trail.

This increased the danger of the Creek scout seeing that he was being followed.

Before long Logan began to suspect the Indian had spotted him. The tracks ahead cut away from the stream for the first time, angling up a rugged incline toward a high, long cliff. As Logan left the stream behind and approached the cliff he saw the farthest tracks led into a break in a massive outcropping of rock.

He slowed his horse and studied the overhang through the lightly falling snow. There didn't seem to be any way out. His hunch that the Indian was laying an ambush for him began to pluck more doggedly at his nerves.

Although he knew he could be wrong, he'd learned long ago that it was healthier to have all your wrong hunches on the safe side. Laying the reins against the buckskin's neck, Logan angled the horse away from the

The Twisted Trail 149

direction of the Creek scout's trail, aiming for a place nearer to the rock's outcropping.

He held his horse to a walk until just within accurate rifle distance of the rocks. It crossed his mind the difficulty of aiming his rifle through the falling snow. Then, abruptly, Logan wrenched the reins right, kicked hard with his heels, and kept kicking. The buckskin leapt to its right and broke into a flat, all-out gallop. A split second later a rifle shot cracked out, much too late. A spout of snow rose and collapsed yards behind the speeding horse.

Hunched over the saddle, Logan kept his horse racing for all it was worth, wrenching it to the left, then to the right, in an unpredictable zigzag course.

Twice more the Creek fired at him. One shot kicked up snow under the buckskin's belly. The other zinged over his back. Seconds after the last shot Logan pulled his horse to a halt under a shielding overhang at the base of the outcropping. The only thing the Creek's shots had accomplished was to let Logan know his position.

Without pausing, Logan slid from his horse and sprinted to the left until he reached a tight little gully leading upward. He climbed rapidly, hugging the bottom of the gully to conceal himself below the shallow sides. He understood that just as he knew the Indian's position, the Creek had a good idea of where Logan was. And the Creek was bound to be swift in changing his position too.

By the time the gully came to an end under a big spur of rock, Logan was sure of one thing; his enemy was still somewhere to his right. He scanned the convoluted and haphazard formations as much as possible without showing himself. The Indian was nowhere in sight, and there were dozens of nooks and crannies where he could hide.

Logan didn't like the idea of playing a hide-and-seek duel. The man higher up always had the advantage, the better chance of spotting the man below first.

He hesitated.

Then, instead of continuing upward, he crawled under the spur and began working his way to the right. He moved with infinite caution, seeking the protection of overhead ledges and projections, pausing every few seconds to look behind him and through cracks and openings above.

Where necessary he squeezed himself under giant fists of rock or crawled through narrow fissures—always conscious that the Creek might suddenly appear where he wasn't looking, with a clear shot of him. Logan was aware of an intensifying sensation of numbness in the small of his back, as though the nerves there were preparing themselves for the expected sudden impact of a fast-moving chunk of lead.

If anything, he knew his enemy would be under the very same strain. They were each both hunter and hunted.

When he was several yards past the area where the Creek had fired at him, Logan stopped and studied the rocks above. If his calculations were right, his man was somewhere up there, and looking in the other direction from him. If so, there was a chance of coming up be-

The Twisted Trail 151

hind him without being spotted. Uncomfortable ifs, but ones by which he would have to live or die.

Logan worked his way upward, the carbine gripped tight in his right hand. He found a tight, jagged seam in the face of the rock leading upward and used it. He climbed slowly, careful not to make a sound. The way became steeper and he had to search for holds for his feet and left hand. He gripped his carbine with his free hand, using his right elbow as leverage, which slowed his progress still more.

Having to hang on to barely nothing to keep from falling, he was sharply conscious of how defenseless he'd be in the vital first split second if the Creek scout spotted him.

Relief flowed through Logan when he finally reached the upper end of the seam. While he rested on a narrow ledge under a massive shoulder of rock, he breathed through bared teeth until the action of his lungs became less violent. In spite of the cold, he wiped sweat from his eyes.

A tangle of rock formation lay in front of him. Logan rose to his feet and started working his way to the left, crouching so low that his chest almost touched his knees. He placed his feet with care so as not to set any of the snow shifting downward to betray his position. He came to a twisted stone pinnacle that barred his way.

As he moved around and under a high ledge, a dusting of snow fell on his hat and shoulders.

As Logan whipped partway around, his right foot

152 *L. W. Rogers*

scraped on bare rock under it. The carbine smacked to his shoulder as he brought it up to fire at the ledge above.

Except for a slight stirring of wind, nothing up there moved.

Logan had barely turned back to his original position when the Indian materialized three feet in front of him. The Creek stepped out from the other side of the stone pinnacle, bringing his rifle around for a point-blank shot at Logan as he made the step. Logan had no time to bring his own carbine to bear.

In the same instant that the Creek appeared, Logan instinctively did the only thing left to him. He wrenched himself forward, swinging the carbine in a swift, vicious arc like a club, putting all the power of his shoulders into the swing. The butt of the carbine thudded against the side of the warrior's neck.

The boom of the Creek's rifle and the sound of his neck snapping as he was knocked sideways against the pinnacle came together.

Hot lead seared Logan's side three inches below his armpit.

The Indian crumpled like a puppet with all of its strings broken. Logan stared down at the Creek's inert form. Dizziness swirled in Logan's head as he sucked wind into his lungs. The dizziness lasted a second, then it was over. His brain steadied and legs that had begun to tremble ceased to do so. He relaxed his grip on the carbine and straightened, looking out and down at the land below.

The Twisted Trail   153

He'd avenged Jake Randall's death. All too soon, before the Indian had led Logan to the rest of his band.

Logan made his way back down to the stream. He found Jake's horse and took him along, releasing the Indian pony to wander off. He realized darkness had closed in around him, and unless he and Joe Panther had been wrong about how close the Creek party was . . . he slouched in the saddle, too tired to think.

He wasn't worried about the other Creeks finding the pony or their dead companion. By then the tracks leading back toward Clarissa's wagons would have been long obliterated. Mounting his buckskin and tugging Jake's horse along by a lead rope he continued to follow the upward course of the stream. He rode warily, knowing it was more than an even chance the other Creeks had heard the rifle shot.

After a half-hour's riding north of the Creek scout he'd killed, he spotted a tendril of smoke rising ahead. Instantly turning away from the stream, Logan rode into a stand of pine. Hidden within the timber, he pushed on in the same direction. Under the protection of the heavy overhanging boughs, he let the buckskin go slow, feeling its way around tangles of underbrush.

When the trees began to thin out on a steep incline, the smoke was on Logan's left, between him and the stream. He kneed his horse up the slope, tugging on the reins of Jake's horse. Higher up the timber became sparse and stunted, the incline became irregular with large, sharp

154   *L. W. Rogers*

up-thrustings of rock. Logan reached the top of the slope between two of the rock thrusts . . . and found himself looking down at the Creek camp.

It was near the stream—a rough, temporary resting place with two slapdash shelters fashioned of pine and balsam boughs leaning against stakes sticking up out of the ground. One warrior carried wood past the ponies to a newly built cook fire.

Logan counted the other men—eleven in all. There were no women.

From the absence of women and children, the fit look of each warrior, and the transient nature of their camp, Logan figured this was a raiding party, out for blood and loot. He doubted the Indians would try a full attack on Clarissa's wagons, even if they chanced to find them. They might try sniping, though there would be nothing to gain by it other than enjoyment.

From experience, Logan knew that as long as no wagon fell behind and no man strayed away as Jake had done, the Indians were likely to leave the wagon train alone. It had too many men, and with every teamster armed the odds were against the small band of warriors.

Judging from the size of the two shelters, even if all the raiding party weren't in the camp at the moment, there could be more than a couple others—not including the one he'd killed.

Still the Indians could make trouble if they happened to discover the wagon train.

Logan was about to turn away when another warrior climbed into view over the crest of a ridge off to the

The Twisted Trail   155

right. At the same moment the newcomer glanced over and spotted Logan.

The Creek yelled his warning to the camp below as Logan whirled his buckskin around, tugging Jake's horse after him. Clarissa's wagon train was off to the west. Logan raced to the east, toward the other pass.

He hadn't gotten far before he heard the Creeks' ponies thundering after him.

Chapter Fourteen

Joe Panther picked the campsite for Clarissa's wagons as dusk closed in. He chose a place against a high, perpendicular cliff, with no timber or sizable rocks close enough to be used as camouflage by anyone planning a night attack.

After the mules were corralled within the square of wagons, Tully Hayes set about preparing the evening meal. Joe Panther said, "Quick meals tonight, Tully. Don't want no fires to reveal our position. Just in case—"

"Dang blast it, Joe Panther. Sneakin' up on a man like that. Near scared the wits outta me."

Joe Panther chuckled at the old cowboy's startled outburst. As a sort of peace offering, he helped Hayes bank the cook fire.

Clarissa stood by the fire, gazing anxiously to the east. "Why hasn't Matt come back yet?" The question seemed

The Twisted Trail   157

more an expression of her fears than a query directed to Joe Panther. "He should have come back by now."

"Most likely he found that Creek Indian," Joe Panther said, with more gentleness than he ever used with any of the men, "and decided to trail him."

"But we need him here."

"We also need to know where the rest of them Creeks are and how many."

"What about Jake Randall?" Clarissa paused. She gave Joe Panther a worried look. "He hasn't come back either."

"Could be he went along with Logan," Joe Panther lied, "to help in case Logan ran into trouble."

Tully Hayes glanced at Joe Panther, saying nothing but knowing as well as Joe Panther that it wasn't so.

The fear that flicked across Clarissa's face showed that she knew it too.

After the evening meal, Clarissa settled down in her bedroll. She thought of Jake Randall's cheerful, pug-nosed face. She found herself thinking of him already as someone in the past, not as someone who still lived.

In spite of her thoughts, weariness took over. She fell asleep—a restless, troubled sleep.

While she slept, Joe Panther picked the best positions to place guards, then assigned the three-men guard duties for the night.

One of the guards asked, "What be the reason for pickin' this place?"

"Call it logic, maybe instinct or both," Joe Panther

158 *L. W. Rogers*

pointed to the steep-walled side of the pass. "Cain't get to us from those steep walls. Anyone wanting to attack will have to come through that pass. Gives us a natural advantage. Satisfied?"

The teamster merely grunted his satisfaction before taking his assigned position for his watch.

After making sure the fires were properly doused, Joe Panther checked the mules before settling down in his own bedroll. He left instructions with Tully Hayes to wake him in three hours.

It was still snowing when Joe Panther awakened Reese Stone to take his turn at guard duty. Stone picked up his rifle and moved through the midnight darkness to take up his position. He shook off the last vestiges of sleep, his mind sharply alert as he mulled over his plans.

He'd thought out his tactics nights ago, after Clarissa had made it obvious she found him repulsive, that she'd played him for a fool before they'd left Fort Brooke. The thought grated on his ego. No woman suckered him.

Carl Sullivan had offered him three times the pay to switch sides. Stone made his decision. There was just one thing to do before he left. He cautioned himself. Patience . . . patience.

His waiting paid off. Besides himself, only two other men stood guard. He figured the falling snow would wipe out his tracks before anyone began tracking him at dawn.

Stone wanted more than three times the money

The Twisted Trail 159

Sullivan offered, much more. He'd deliver Clarissa to Sullivan as a hostage.

Stone waited. He watched the dark shapeless forms of sleeping men on the ground by the wagons. He knew the positions of Joe Panther and the other guard. He was sure he could accomplish what he had to before either of them noticed.

Stone allowed a half hour. Then he left his guard position and slipped away in a low crouch toward the spot where he'd watched Clarissa bed down. He moved slowly and quietly, making no sound as he approached her.

He stopped a few feet away to study the way her dark form lay in the shadows, locating the position of her head barely showing out of the blanket wrapped around her. Then he drew one of his Colts and tiptoed closer. He bent over her, raised the gun a few inches, then whipped it sharply against the side of her head.

She quivered, not coming out of her sleep, then rolled on to her back and lay still. Stone knew the amount of force to use. The blow couldn't do much damage. He figured she'd remain unconscious long enough for him to get away with her.

Stone glanced around and saw no sign that he'd been seen or heard. Sliding the Colt back into its holster, he stripped the blanket from Clarissa. She'd bedded down fully dressed, even to her boots. He slipped his arms under her thighs and back and lifted her from the ground.

Carrying her inert weight proved more strenuous than Stone had figured. His breath came in short pants

160   *L. W. Rogers*

when he got to one of the openings between the wagons. He lowered Clarissa to the ground by a wagon wheel. It took a moment to get his breath back. He shook with cold as he untied the ropes that stretched between the two wagons and slipped inside. He walked to his horse, making as little noise as possible. Before bedding down, he'd placed his gear close to the wagon wheel. With quick, efficient movements, he saddled the horse, then slid his rifle into the scabbard.

As he led the horse forward, a quiet voice stopped Stone in his tracks. "What the hell're you up to?"

Stone turned quickly. His hand touched the gun on his right hip. He cursed himself for having become too preoccupied to notice one of the guards approach. The teamster didn't act suspicious, only puzzled.

Stone kept his voice low. "Thought I saw something move back down the pass. I'm going for a look."

"By yourself? Shouldn't you . . ." The words trailed off as the teamster glanced downward and saw Clarissa heaped in an unconscious bundle. "What the—"

Stone already had his gun in hand. Before the man could react, Stone slashed the pistol across the man's temple. The teamster managed a shout before the gun barrel struck. Even as he fell, dark figures rose up off the ground to their knees and hands, as men were jerked from their sleep by the sound.

It seemed the camp exploded around him. There was no longer time to get Clarissa's horse. Stone bent quickly and grabbed up her sprawled figure. He slung her across his horse in front of the saddle. The next

The Twisted Trail 161

second, he swung onto the horse and raced down the pass.

Before anyone in the camp figured out what had happened, Stone had ridden out of sight with Clarissa still unconscious.

Logan rode into the other pass with the Creek Indians racing after him. He pushed his buckskin hard. Snow piled deeper. The horse stumbled getting through heavy drifts. Once Logan almost had to let go of the rope that pulled Jake Randall's horse behind him. His head start on his pursuers and the ground snow slowed them too.

He reached the other side of the pass. He kept out of rifle range by working his way up the timbered slope. Once there, he sped on to the east, leading the Indians off in the opposite direction from Clarissa's wagon train. He kept riding due east until nightfall.

With the coming of dark, Logan turned north, rode into a thick stand of timber, and pulled his horse to a halt. The buckskin pawed the snowy ground as if anxious to keep moving. Logan leaned forward and almost crooned to the animal. "I hear 'em, Buck. Stand quiet."

The horse settled to Logan's voice.

Minutes later Logan heard the sounds of the Creeks' ponies going past his hiding place, though he couldn't see them. His own horse quivered beneath him. He rubbed his hand down Buck's neck to quiet the horse.

Logan waited until the sounds faded out to the east of him. Then he climbed down from the buckskin. He knew the horse was run-out. Switching to Jake's horse, he brought the buckskin along by the lead rope. Logan rode out of the thicket and struck toward the south.

He looked up at the sky. With the night, the falling snow, and the bloated clouds blotting out the stars and moon, there was no danger of the Creeks finding his trail. By dawn there'd be none of his tracks left in the area to tell the Indians he'd changed directions.

Logan continued south for a time. Then he turned west, crossing the other pass, then heading back to where his outfit waited. His body ached and he needed sleep.

By the time he neared the wagon camp it had stopped snowing. The overcast clouds broke apart and separated into smaller clouds. A sure sign the snow was over for a while.

He rode within hailing distance. "Hello, the camp."

"Who goes there?"

Logan called out again, identifying himself. As he rode into the camp, it surprised him to see the entire crew up. Before he had both feet on the ground, he asked, "Something happen? Indians?"

The teamster that Stone had whacked on the head spoke up and told him about Clarissa. "Far as I could tell, she was unconscious. Stone must've knocked her out. Soon's I seen her laying there I started to yell. Next thing I know, I was comin' to on the ground with a headache the size of a watermelon."

"We went after him," Tully Hayes said. "But he lost us. And it was too dark to find his trail."

Logan stood silent for a moment. He seemed to gather

The Twisted Trail 163

himself up out of his weariness. He drew a hand across his haggard face. When he spoke his voice was as hard and flat as his stare.

"Where's Joe Panther?"

Hayes used a rag to lift the burbling coffeepot from the fire. He poured a cup and handed it to Logan. "He told the rest of us to get on back to camp."

"Which way'd he go?"

Tully pointed south with his thumb. "Back down the pass. He reckoned Stone must've cut off from it somewhere." Tully set the coffeepot on a rock next to the fire. "Stone's carryin' double. Reckon we'd a caught him if'n he'd stuck to the pass."

Logan blew at the steaming liquid before taking a sip. Tully Hayes spoke. "Stone made a mistake. He figured the snow'd cover his tracks. Only now it's stopped snowin' and he'll be cuttin' a clear trail. If you hadn't showed up, me and a few of the boys figured to circle around back there 'til we found his back trail and—"

"How long before it stopped snowing did Stone head out?" Logan cut in.

"'bout two hours. Mebbe less."

Logan swallowed the last of his coffee. "Take a lot of time to find where his tracks start. You and the men stay in camp. Keep an eye on things."

Hayes shifted from his twisted leg to rest on his good one. "Noticed you brought in Jake's horse. Jake?"

Logan told them how he'd found Jake and the Creek Indians. "We're well to the west of them, and in a few days we'll be well north of them. In the meanwhile,

164 *L. W. Rogers*

they could find us and make enough trouble to keep the wagons from moving, especially if too many men are off hunting Stone. I'll go after him. Try to catch up to Joe Panther."

He fought the fatigue invading his body. "Tully, wrangle me up some food and coffee. A lot of it."

"Your feet're gonna fall out from under you if you don't get some shut-eye."

Logan repeated himself. "Fix me a meal. And coffee."

Tully Hayes turned to do so without another word.

To the man nearest him, Logan said, "Saddle me two fresh horses. Give mine and Jake's an extra handful of oats. They've earned it."

The teamster looked dubious. "One man alone will take a helluva long time to find Stone's back trail."

Logan rubbed his hands restlessly against his thighs. "I won't be hunting for his back trail. If I'm thinking straight, he's headed for Sullivan's outfit. Stone figures Sullivan will pay a tidy sum to get Clarissa in his hands. He could force her to sell her freight to him, at his price, with a legal written contract. And use her to make us hand over the wagons."

Hayes nodded slowly. "Could be. So you figure he'll head down the south pass to meet up with Sullivan's wagon train. And all you got to do is ride the same trail, only faster."

"You said his horse is carrying double." Logan spoke through clenched teeth. "I'll have two horses. If I catch sight of Sullivan's wagons without coming across Joe Panther or Stone's track, it'll be because I've passed

The Twisted Trail 165

both of them. If so, I'll turn back and keep looking. One way or the other, I'm going to get to Stone before he gets to Sullivan."

Joe Panther trudged through the snow and into camp on foot, his saddle slung over his shoulder. He walked over to one of the wagons and tossed his saddle and bridle into the back of a wagon. Then he joined Logan and the rest of the men.

Logan nodded his greeting. "Where's your horse?"

"Snow covered a hole. Horse stepped in it. Broke his leg."

"Didn't hear a shot."

"Nope. Didn't figure to alert the entire Creek nation. Used my knife."

"Too bad about your horse."

"Yeah. He was a good pony." Joe Panther squatted to the fire to warm his hands.

Logan waited for the Seminole to speak.

"Stone's headed straight for Sullivan's camp. Guess you figured that out."

"Uh-huh."

"Get some sleep, friend. You won't do Clarissa much good if you're too tired to shoot straight." Joe Panther continued to warm his hands.

"Nope."

"Stone's carrying double, through deep snow." He seemed to size Logan up for a moment. "Suit yourself."

Tully Hayes walked over with a plate of hot beans and bacon. Logan made himself eat all it. He hadn't eaten since noon, but he had no appetite. He was plumb worn out from riding and there was more riding to do. He gulped down scalding hot coffee without tasting or feeling it, held out the cup for a refill, and drank that down too before he finished the last of his food.

Hayes poured him a third cup. Logan said, "Fix me a food bag. Enough for two days."

"I already did. Biscuits, salt beef, and cooked beans. And your canteen's filled too."

Logan drank the rest of the coffee. "Joe Panther, I need you to stay here. Never know when the Creek Indians will figure out my back trail and find the camp. You'll know what to do."

Joe Panther voiced one last objection. "I still don't like you goin' it alone after Stone. He's one real deadly breed of snake."

Logan's angry voice drawled, "I've killed snakes before."

Chapter Fifteen

Several hours after noon, Reese Stone came to a place where the land heaved up in a series of snow-covered hills that separated two mountain slopes a mile apart. He walked, leading his tired horse and pushing Clarissa ahead of him. Apparently ready to collapse, she stumbled with every other step.

Stone's own legs felt heavy. His horse needed to rest from carrying extra weight. Stone decided to let the animal have another fifteen minutes. Better to give it a breather than to have to walk the long distance to Sullivan's camp. He didn't care if the horse died from the effort as long as it got them to Sullivan.

He pushed up the slope of a hill, prodding Clarissa's back with his fist to keep her moving. She staggered up ahead of him, each step an obvious effort. When she reached the crest of the hill, her legs gave way and she

168 *L. W. Rogers*

sank down into the snow. Drawing up her legs, she wrapped her arms around them and rested her forehead on her knees.

Stone stopped beside her. He gazed toward the south pass, hoping to see Sullivan's wagons coming toward him. They weren't in sight. His fingers nervously caressed the butt of one pistol. He turned and looked back the way he'd come. The sight of the tracks he'd clearly left behind caused him concern.

"Didn't figure on it to stop snowing so soon."

Clarissa raised her head. "What?"

"Nothing." He snarled.

He consoled himself with the thought that Logan and his Seminole sidekick wouldn't be able to track him until dawn. Even then it was bound to take them a couple of hours to find where his trail started. He still had plenty of time to get to Sullivan's outfit before Logan caught up to him. And he counted on that.

Stone looked down at Clarissa. His voice as cold as the snow, he said, "Get up and get moving."

Her head remained on her knees. She gave no sign that she'd heard him.

"I said get up." He nudged her in the back with the toe of his boot.

Clarissa raised her head. She made no effort to move. "I can't. I have to rest."

"You'll rest later," Stone told her in that peculiar, empty voice of his. "Don't make me repeat myself, Clarissa." As an afterthought, he added, "If I had the

The Twisted Trail   169

time, I'd teach you how to obey. You're long overdue for a rough lesson."

She almost smiled. "But you don't have the time, do you? You're scared stiff of what Logan will do when he catches you—"

His hand moved too fast for her to avoid the slap. The sharp sound of his palm against her cheek was loud. Clarissa fell over on her side and lay there looking up at him.

He wanted her to be afraid, looked for the fear in her eyes. Instead he saw hatred.

"You'll either get up," he told her, "or I'll start kicking you. Hard!"

She swayed on her feet as she stood.

Clarissa wasn't as weary as she looked. Shortly after leaving the camp and when she'd regained consciousness, she had decided to do whatever it took to slow Stone's progress. Picking a place where the snow looked deep and soft, she had fallen off the horse. This forced Stone to stop, climb down, and pick her up. Then she'd pretended to be semi-conscious, going limp to make it harder for him to get her and himself back on the horse.

Five minutes later, she'd repeated the act. After that he'd had to give much of his attention to holding her to keep her from sliding off the horse.

The rest of the time she rode, Clarissa leaned as much of her weight forward as she could against the

170 *L. W. Rogers*

horse's neck to tire the animal faster. When she walked, she staggered.

She staggered now as Stone pushed her ahead of him. At the bottom of the slope she dropped to her knees, head sagging.

Disgusted with her, Stone said, "I meant what I said about kicking you."

"I'm too exhausted to go much farther. It doesn't matter what you do to me." Her lips twisted in a hateful smile. "Besides, if you kick me to death you won't have anything to bargain with. I'm no good to Sullivan dead."

Stone hauled Clarissa to her feet. He yanked her to him so that she smelled his fetid breath. She raised her head, meeting his shadowed, unreadable eyes.

"I won't kill you," he told her, "but you're no different than your mules when they feel the sting of the whip. You'd be surprised how a little pain can make you keep going longer than you think you can."

She rose to her feet. They walked through a short, narrow opening between two hilly slopes. As they came out the other side, a voice stopped Stone in his tracks.

Logan said behind them, "Stand right where you are."

Clarissa didn't wait for Logan to tell her what to do. She dropped to the ground leaving Stone an exposed target. He whirled around, his hand flashing to the butts of his pistols. He stopped himself with the guns halfway out of their holsters. He forced his fingers to spread open, letting the two Colts slide back into place in their holsters.

Logan leaned against the side of a notch in the hill's

The Twisted Trail 171

slope, holding his carbine trained on Stone's middle. Behind him, deeper inside the notch, stood his two horses.

Logan straightened a bit. "Now unbuckle your gunbelt."

Stone remained frozen in position, hands still poised over the grips of his guns. He noted the dull shine to Logan's eyes. "You look like a man in need of sleep, Logan."

He focused on Stone's eyes. He didn't answer.

Stone held his voice tight. "You're wearing a gun on your hip. Put the rifle down, and we'll both have an even chance."

"Not so even," Logan said. "You made the mistake of showing me how fast you are."

"You saying you're afraid of me?"

"Yep. I'm afraid. Now either go for your guns or drop them. You've got two seconds to decide."

Stone stared at the round dark eye of the carbine aimed at his stomach. His hands went to the buckles of his gunbelts, unfastened them and let them fall to the snow.

"Now kick them away from you," Logan spoke in a monotone.

Stone hesitated, then hooked a toe under each gunbelt and kicked them away. "You going to shoot me down?"

"If I was, I'd already done it."

Clarissa rose to her feet. Logan glanced at the hand imprint on her face. "Did he hurt you much?"

She touched her cheek. "I didn't enjoy it. If you were near enough to hear why didn't you stop him?"

172   *L. W. Rogers*

"Needed the element of surprise." Logan seethed inside at the thought of Stone hitting her.

She gave Logan a faint smile—one that indicated she understood.

God, how beautiful she was in spite of her tousled hair and her nose red from the cold. And the expression that had crept into her face when she'd turned at the sound of his voice. It was with determined effort that he drew his attention away from her when Stone's voice interrupted his thoughts.

"A duel."

"Huh-uh."

"You *are* yellow." Stone's lips formed a hateful smile.

Logan told Clarissa in a lazy voice, "Move farther away from him."

She obeyed immediately, watching them.

Logan motioned to Stone by raising the carbine an inch. "Back up three steps."

Like a man in a trance, not knowing what came next, Stone backed away. Logan moved to Stone's horse, drew the rifle from its saddle scabbard and checked it. He levered a cartridge into the chamber and thrust the rifle back into the scabbard. Then he backed off into the notch in the hillside and brought out one of his horses.

"Come back beside your horse," he told Stone.

The puzzled look disappeared from the killer's face. He moved up beside his saddle with all of his usual fluid smoothness. Logan unbuckled his own gunbelt and let it drop. Then he slid his carbine into the saddleboot of the

The Twisted Trail   173

horse beside him. He faced Stone with empty hands. Something savage glowed in the depths of blue eyes that were no longer sleepy.

"Understand now?"

Stone understood but said, "No."

"You wanted to try your speed against mine. Let's try it with something neither of us have spent practicing."

Now Clarissa spoke. "Don't, Matt. He'll—"

Stone's reptilian eyes cut her off. They flicked contemptuously from Logan to Clarissa. He said nothing. Then he took a coiled-spring step and twisted toward his horse to whip the rifle from its scabbard. It took him a split second to bring the rifle to bear on Logan.

In that same split second, Logan fired.

The bullet struck Stone in the center of his chest. The impact spun him completely around, his finger still on the trigger when he again faced Logan. The bullet went high when he pulled the trigger.

Logan, holding the carbine hip-high, fired again. The weapon jerked in his hands. This time Stone fell backwards in the snow. His arms and legs sprawled out from his body. His mouth opened for its last breath and he stared at the sky with eyes that couldn't see.

Logan rolled his shoulders as though easing a knot between them.

He unfastened one hand from the carbine and lowered it. Exhaustion seeped through every inch of his body. He watched the stoic tautness crumple from Clarissa's face. He opened his arms to her.

174   *L. W. Rogers*

Like a whirlwind, she stepped past Stone's frozen, immobile body and into Logan's arms. She went to him swearing and crying at the same time.

There were questions in his mind, hiding there stubbornly even when he didn't want to think about them. Not the least of them, he now had to admit to himself unwillingly, that he had feelings for Clarissa that went beyond friendship.

He pushed her away from him, gave her a frowning, brooding look before he said in an ordinary voice, "His horse looks done in."

"It is," her voice still shaky.

"Then we'll leave it here with him." Logan handed Clarissa his carbine. He walked over to the animal, unsaddled it, and dumped Stone's gear in the snow. "Reckon Sullivan's group'll be along in about three hours. He can claim it . . . and the body."

He took the carbine back from Clarissa and slipped it into its saddle scabbard. "But take his rifle," he said in the same even tone. "It might come in handy."

That night, Logan and Clarissa made a cold camp deep in the mountains. They shared the beans, hard biscuits, and salt beef from Logan's food bag and washed it down with water. Logan ate slow, finding he was too tired to chew. Finally he gave up.

"I'm done in," he announced in a dull voice, as much to himself as to Clarissa.

"How long has it been since you've slept?"

"Two days and a night of riding." He hunkered down

The Twisted Trail   175

inside his bedroll and pulled his battered Stetson down over his face. "We'll sleep here, then push on at dawn."

"If it helps any," she said, her voice a mere whisper, "I appreciate your coming after me."

She listened to the soft patter of his breath and knew he had fallen asleep.

Clarissa bedded down in her own blankets. She looked over at Logan's shadowy figure in the faint starlight filtering through the pine boughs. Her mind warned. *Be careful . . . be careful.* It would be far too easy to slip between his blankets now, to put her arms around him, touch his hair where it curled at the nape of his neck, touch her lips to his. She shivered—as much from the cold as from the emotions building inside of her.

It was as if he'd read her thoughts when he said, "You cold?"

Her lips quirked. "Yes."

In the starlight she saw him lift one side of the top blanket a bit. "There's room enough. And we'll both sleep warmer."

Clarissa sighed. "I was hoping you'd offer." She gathered her own bedroll and spread it over the top of his. She slid between the blankets with him, their bodies just touching.

Logan turned his head and studied her face inches from his. "You still look all tense."

She smiled at him. "Sometimes it takes awhile to let go."

176   *L. W. Rogers*

He looked at her thoughtfully. "I suppose I could help." He gathered her into his arms, bringing all her soft warmth against him. "After all, you did earn this much . . ." There was a trace of amusement in his voice, and something else. His hand slid behind her neck, fingers feeling their way through her hair.

"You have beautiful hair, Clarissa. It feels like silk."

She made a soft, mewling sound in her throat, as his hands found her.

His breath became a thick fog in his own throat. "Don't do anything you'll be sorry for in the morning, Clarissa."

"I . . . want to know you, Matt," she whispered with her lips moving on his, "to know more . . ."

By the time Logan and Clarissa broke camp the next morning and started north again, her wagon train was being destroyed.

Chapter Sixteen

Beams of late afternoon light stabbed through the pine trees. Logan pointed upward. "Buzzards."

He and Clarissa rode north up the pass on the trail of her wagons. She looked up at the buzzards wheeling lazily around an area up ahead. "Wonder what it means?"

Logan eyed the carrion birds. Without saying anything, he moved his horse along faster. Clarissa kept pace with him, watching the buzzards. A chill that had nothing to do with the weather raced through her.

As soon as they reached the place where the buzzards hovered, Clarissa let out a little gasp. The pass where they stood held high, steep walls, supported only by an occasional dwarf pine or scrub oak. Down in the pass between the high walls was what was left of her wagon train.

178 *L. W. Rogers*

Clarissa gripped the reins of her pinto. The pony snorted and sidestepped. She made shushing sounds to settle the nervous animal as she followed Logan into the camp.

One wagon lay over on its side in the middle of the pass, a hunk of granite protruded through a broken back wheel. Dead mules lay around it. To one side the rest of the wagons had been formed into a rough corral with the surviving mules roaming restlessly inside it.

Nearby, a group of men were busy digging two graves. They straightened and stood, shovels in hand, bleakly watching Logan and Clarissa approach.

Logan pulled his buckskin to a halt. He looked at the two bodies stretched out on the ground between the grave holes. Both were the new men he'd hired back in Fort Brooke.

Joe Panther limped toward Logan, one trouser bullet-ripped and blood-stained. A surviving teamster cradled a broken arm. Another had a bullet-gashed cheek and a torn ear.

Tully Hayes looked miserably at Clarissa as she dismounted. " 'Fraid I let you down, Miz Hubbard."

Clarissa thought he'd aged since she and Logan had last seen him. She looked about at the carnage. Her voice trembled. "How did this happen?"

Logan answered for Hayes. "Easy enough." He tried to contain the harshness in his voice. "With me and Reese Stone gone and Jake dead, that left only Joe Panther to ride guard."

Tully Hayes nodded and drew a bony hand across his

The Twisted Trail 179

mouth as if wiping away a taste he didn't like. "They was up on that ridge there," he told them, pointing. "From their fire, I judged seven of 'em. Must've got in position during the night. We rode right into it just after breakin' camp this morning. Dang their ornery hides . . . they concentrated on the mules."

Logan glanced around at the dead animals. "How many, Tully?"

"Twenty-one."

Joe Panther spoke up. "I had a look at Sullivan's wagon train yesterday. From a long way off, but I'm dang sure there weren't seven men missing from his crew. Anyway, they couldn't spare that many and still handle all their wagons."

Logan slapped his hand against his leather chaps. "Which means Sullivan went and got himself some more men."

Clarissa turned her dazed eyes to him. "Where? Where could he get more men around here?"

"From Dahlonega. Mules pulling heavy wagons move a lot slower than men riding horses. Sullivan could easily get to Dahlonega, hire six new men, and get back down here with them in time for our wagons to enter the pass."

"He sure picked 'em," Tully Hayes rasped. "All good rifle shots. Soon's Joe Panther heard the shots, he come ridin' into camp like a group of wild Comanches were on his tail. Anyhow, him and me and a coupla others went up there after 'em. We got one. Found his body."

"Yeah," Joe Panther said, "the rest cut and rode off. Guess they figured they'd done what Sullivan had paid them for." He shook his head ruefully. "We'll have a helluva time tryin' to get all this freight through now. We only got enough mules left to pull five wagons."

Logan asked, "Tully, we got a spare wheel for that one over there?"

"Yep. But if we spread the mules thin to pull all eight wagons, it'll be slow going. And even if we do pile all the freight on five wagons, it'd be the same thing. Wagons will be too heavy for the mules to pull much faster than a crawl."

Joe Panther looked up at the gray sky. "From the looks of that, we're in for heavy snow. Won't take long for every pass to fill too deep to get through. We won't make it, pulling that slow."

"Then we'll have to leave three of the loaded wagons behind." The men had almost forgotten about Clarissa until she spoke. "We can come back for them after we get the other five to Dahlonega."

"Same trouble," Logan told her. "Snow will close the pass before we can get back. The wagons will be stuck here all winter. By spring, Indians will have picked 'em clean."

Clarissa felt as if she'd already put up with too much for the past two days. By this time, she was past caring. She had been kidnapped, kicked, and her life threatened. Feeling a wave of cynical self-pity, she looked up and met Logan's eyes for a moment. They seemed like the dark, opaque blue eyes of a stranger, weighing her, calculating how much further use she might have of him after all this was over.

The Twisted Trail   181

Her shoulders slumped as she sighed. "Then I'll have to take the loss. There's nothing else we can do."

"There's one thing . . ." Logan took his time as he spoke. His right hand idly smoothed itself against the leather of his holster as he gazed south. "We can get ourselves some more mules."

Clarissa frowned at him. "Mules? Where?"

"From Sullivan."

Tully Hayes gave him a dubious scowl. "How? We ain't got enough crew left to tackle Sullivan's outfit. With those new men he hired he's plain got too many guns for us. And this time he'll expect us . . . and be ready."

Clarissa watched the brooding, preoccupied expression on Logan's face. He said, "Uh-huh, we'll divide and conquer."

Hayes's face showed only puzzlement. "Speak English."

Logan grinned. "Something I learned when I was scouting for the cavalry. 'Course, we'll need help doing it."

He looked at Joe Panther. "In about another day, Sullivan will be almost as far north as we are."

Joe Panther nodded his understanding. "In that pass over there. And he'll be a lot nearer to where those hostile Creeks are camped than we are."

Hayes caught on to the idea. His grin was nasty. "That ain't such a bad idea."

"Not bad at all," Logan agreed. Before he started toward the graves, he laid a thoughtful hand on Clarissa's

182   *L. W. Rogers*

shoulder. "You're all done in, Clarissa. Get some rest. You've earned it."

Almost absentmindedly, she wiped the sleeve of her jacket across her face. Her voice sounded childish when she whispered, "Yes." She whirled and almost ran to the wagon.

She heard him say, "Let's get the burying done."

When the two teamsters lay under their mounds of earth and piled stone, the overturned wagon had its broken wheel replaced and was heaved upright. The men hitched the mules that were left to pull five wagons a mile farther up the pass, away from the dead mules. Then the other three freight wagons and the chuck wagon were brought up.

By the time the new camp was set up, Clarissa had rested. She stepped out of the wagon and strolled to the campfire where Logan sat. She accepted a cup of coffee from Tully Hayes. For a moment she stared into the smoldering embers.

She turned to Logan. "Now what?"

"Now," he said, "we wait." He drew a deck of playing cards from his jacket pocket and began to shuffle them with careless ease between his strong hands. "Anybody care for some poker?"

Twenty-four hours later, Logan stood on a high-timbered slope. He watched Sullivan's wagon train come up the pass below him.

Logan was alone. He stood next to his buckskin gelding. Joe Panther and four rifle-armed teamsters waited

The Twisted Trail

183

several miles farther north. They knew what to do if Logan didn't get back to them in time. Clarissa, Tully Hayes, and two other teamsters stayed in camp guarding the wagons.

The slope on which Logan stood was high, but not steep. The pass beneath him was an impassable jumble of rocks and boulders. Beyond him, still farther to the north, a ledge rose higher than his position. And beyond that, the ledge went over a ridge to a wide route down to an unblocked continuation of the pass.

From his vantage point, the wagons and mules below looked the size of toys. He counted the men riding guard. Two rode ahead of the first wagon. Two on each side of the wagons rode flank. Two more rode a hundred yards behind the last wagon.

Eight in all. Logan lifted his field glasses and focused them until the two guards riding point became clear in the lens. One was Driscoll. The other was Novak.

He moved the glasses slowly along the wagons until he found Sullivan, riding flank. Logan put away the glasses and drew his carbine from its scabbard. Then he waited while he watched the wagons move closer up the wide ledge below.

When the lead wagons were almost directly under him, Logan braced himself against a tree trunk and brought the carbine to his shoulder. He sighted down the barrel and took aim at the tiny figure of Driscoll.

The distance was against Logan. His first shot kicked up snow between Driscoll and Novak. Both instantly wheeled their horses toward the slope. Logan quickly

184   *L. W. Rogers*

adjusted the sights. He levered another cartridge into firing position, following Novak with his sights and then leading him a fraction. He fired, levered and fired again, the two shots ringing out one on the other.

Novak spun out of his saddle. He hit the snow and rolled, scrambling to his feet. Catching his shoulder, left arm dangling, Novak threw himself behind a mound by the time Logan levered for another shot.

Logan swung the carbine to fire at Driscoll, who vanished into the timber below before the sights were lined up on him. Cursing, Logan looked for the other guards. They had all disappeared from sight. Which meant they were all in the timber now, working their way up the slope toward him. He figured it was time to leave while the getting was good.

Sliding the carbine back into its scabbard, Logan grabbed the reins and tugged the buckskin after him up the slope. The timber came to an abrupt end. Logan swung into the saddle and kicked the gelding into action. As the horse ran over the bare crest, guns blasted out at Logan from the timber below. Once down the other side and out of sight, he raced west. The buckskin left a clear trail behind in the snow.

Logan looked back over his shoulder without slowing. Five men raced after him. So far so good. Logan figured this meant two men had stayed behind to guard the wagons. He flattened himself against Buck's neck and urged more speed from the horse to get ahead of his pursuers.

The Twisted Trail 185

Logan worried that the five wagon guards might quit and turn back. To urge them on, he twice slowed his horse allowing the men time to get closer. He knew cutting his safe margin thin was dangerous, yet necessary to make them believe their horses were faster than his. If he could make them believe they could run his horse into the ground, then the rest of his plan would work.

The guards continued after him, gradually closing the gap when he rode through a notch and sighted the stream dead ahead of him, a stand of pines on his right. He cut toward the timber and into it. His pursuers made a great deal of noise entering the dense woods behind him.

Logan made his way out the other side of the copse. Between the upthrusting of rock at the top of the incline and looking directly at him, stood a tall Creek warrior.

Without slowing, Logan whipped out his Colt and fired. The shot didn't hit its target. The Indian vanished below the other side of the incline.

Instantly Logan wheeled to the right toward a grouping of boulders leading to a low ridge. Before the five gunmen came in sight behind him, Logan had slid from his horse. Removing his hat, he raised his head just enough to see the incline.

Sullivan's gunmen rode out of the thick timber following his trail. An instant later twelve mounted, rifle-toting Creek Indians boiled up over the other side of the incline's crest.

For a moment both groups reined to a sudden halt as they saw each other. Before the moment ended, rifles

186 *L. W. Rogers*

rang out. Logan saw two Indians and one of Sullivan's men fall. The next instant both groups scattered for cover, firing as they moved.

Leading the buckskin, Logan worked his way upward behind the boulders. In order to keep out of sight, he took many detours. This slowed his progress. When he neared the ridge he allowed himself one last peek over the boulders at the scene below.

A second gunman lay dead, sprawled facedown over a rock. The Creeks were all on foot now, and each had found some form of cover—a tree, a rock, or a hollow in the ground. They had Sullivan's three remaining gunmen pinned down behind a fallen tree.

Logan counted nine Indians. It wasn't likely any of the gunmen would get out alive. He held no sympathy for the gunmen.

When he had the ridge between himself and the sound of battle, Logan swung up into the saddle and rode toward Clarissa's camp.

Chapter Seventeen

Logan found Joe Panther's horse and the horses of the four teamsters tethered in a stand of heavy timber near a narrow trail. He left his gelding with the other horses. With carbine in hand, he headed south on foot through the dense piney woods.

After a mile he found Joe Panther and the teamsters crouching behind a ridge overlooking the pass. The Seminole heard him first. He turned, saw Logan, and almost smiled.

"You're in time for the fun. Sullivan's wagons ain't in sight yet."

Logan frowned. "Hope he hasn't decided to hold up until all his guards get back."

"Nope. I went back down and had a look. He's comin' all right. Reckon Sullivan figured it wasn't safe to hang around the place where you sniped at 'em. 'Specially

188   *L. W. Rogers*

while his wagon train's short on guards." Joe Panther gave Logan a quizzical look. "Any chance of those others getting back?"

"Huh-uh."

Joe Panther looked pleased. "Good."

"You men take care of cutting down those two trees?" Logan looked below at two pines trees that grew from the side of the slope.

The teamster next to him answered, "Sure did. Got 'em secured in position by ropes just like you said."

"And the rocks?"

The man pointed.

Logan nodded his approval. On either side of the trees, also secured by ropes, were two log platforms. Each supported a mass of huge rocks hidden from below by a careful placement of some of the spreading bushes that covered much of the slope.

He looked at his men. "You've been working."

"Yeah," said one of them. "Payback's gonna be hell."

He said it with deep satisfaction.

When Sullivan's wagons started around the bend in the ledge, Logan and his men waited above them, concealed behind the chopped-through pines and the rock platforms.

The first to come into sight was the point rider. Much to Logan's disappointment, the rider was neither Novak nor Sullivan. Which meant that Novak was probably nursing his bullet-broken arm in one of the wagons,

The Twisted Trail 189

and Sullivan was riding drag behind the last of his twelve freight wagons.

The point rider was directly below when the chuck wagon came around the bend. The first of the freight wagons followed, then the second. Tension built in Logan as he waited for the third wagon to pass below him, with the fourth one nearing. He raised his carbine and aimed at the point rider. Joe Panther did the same. They fired at the same time.

The shots hammered the guard from his saddle and flung him over the lip of the ledge toward the pass bottom far below.

At the signal, the teamsters cut all the securing ropes. The two big trees and the released rocks thundered down the steep slope, sending up a huge cloud of snow and dust in their wake. Some of the big rocks bounced off the ledge and kept on going down toward the bottom of the pass. Enough settled on the ledge itself, together with both trees to block the ledge completely. Closed off from the first four, the remaining eight wagons were back around the bend and unable to move any farther.

The driver of the chuck wagon and the men handling the four freight wagons came out of their shock. Yelling back and forth, they snatched up rifles and began firing up the slope.

Logan, his teamsters, and Joe Panther, returned fire. They worked their way down toward the ledge, shooting as they went.

190   *L. W. Rogers*

The chuck wagon driver was shot out of his seat before he could do more than lift his rifle. One of Sullivan's freighters was killed in midair as he leaped toward the ground. Another was smashed off the ledge as he scrambled for cover.

The man driving the fourth freight wagon jumped to the ground, sprinted south, and vanished around the bend. The only Sullivan man still alive dropped his rifle and sidearm. He stepped out from behind his wagon with his hands held high. The first of Logan's teamsters to reach the man knocked him cold with his rifle stock.

By the time Logan and Joe Panther reached the ledge, Logan's men had climbed up on the wagons. The men waited for Logan's signal. While Joe Panther acted as lookout, Logan motioned for the first wagon to move out. Then the second wagon followed the first.

Rifle barrels appeared over the top of the ledge; some heads started to inch up on the other side. Logan and Joe Panther fired simultaneously. The heads ducked back out of sight. Logan motioned for his driver to get the third freight wagon rolling.

After a mile, the drivers halted the wagons. They worked swiftly at unhitching the mules from the wagons, leading the mules in their traces. The same was done with the chuck wagon and its horse team. Then, one by one, the men rolled each of the wagons over the ledge, sending it crashing down into the rocks below.

When the last one had gone over, Logan looked down at the broken wagons and scattered freight. His smile was brief and bleak.

The Twisted Trail   191

Joe Panther sidled up next to Logan. "Dang shame."

"Yeah. I don't take pleasure in waste." Logan turned to help the others in getting the horse and mule teams up the slope.

Joe Panther followed. "Reckon how long it'll take for Sullivan to find a way around that blocked pass?"

"Long enough." Logan's eyes were as grim as the set of his mouth.

Beyond the crest, Logan and his group of men entered a narrow trail though a dense forest. A little farther on they came to where they'd earlier left their saddle horses. The teamsters mounted and continued west, pulling the teams of mules and horses after them by lead ropes back toward Clarissa's camp.

Logan and Joe Panther stayed behind, concealed on either side of the narrow trail, ready to cut down anyone who came riding after them.

"You think Sullivan will send anyone after us?" Joe Panther spoke in a hushed whisper.

"Don't think so. Sullivan's outfit only had a couple of horses left. My guess is he won't find two men willing to commit suicide by attacking a larger number of armed men or strike at Clarissa's wagons."

Joe Panther chuckled. "Yeah. Sullivan now has bigger problems to think on. It's gonna take him a long time to move past those boulders we dumped on the ledge if he wants to continue north. You think he'll try to salvage any of the goods?"

"Sullivan is greedy. He'll try piling as much of the dumped freight as he can on the rest of his wagons.

192 *L. W. Rogers*

And the extra weight will slow his mules considerably."

With that one thing, Logan was satisfied Sullivan wouldn't likely bother them again between here and Dahlonega.

Logan scanned the gray skies and billowing clouds. Clarissa rode her pony up next to Logan. "How much longer to Dahlonega?"

"Four days, mebbe five. Depends on the weather."

Clarissa held the pinto's reins in one hand and used the other to bunch the collar of her coat closer around her throat. "What does Joe Panther say?"

"Could be flurries or worse. Ride inside of the chuck wagon, Clarissa. It'll be warmer." The wind snatched at his words.

Only Logan's eyes showed from beneath his hat. The rest of his face protected by a bandana. He urged Buck into a trot, moving alongside each wagon where he shouted to the drivers, "Keep 'em moving . . . head for that stand of trees."

The deep snow cost them another day.

Three days from Dahlonega, a snowstorm that lasted most of the day brought Clarissa's wagons to a halt.

After the weather cleared, Tully Hayes built a fire. He filled the coffee kettle with snow. When the water came to a boil, he dumped a healthy portion of ground coffee into the pot.

Logan and Joe Panther huddled together. Each

The Twisted Trail 193

stamped their feet against the cold. As soon as Tully Hayes announced the coffee ready, Logan and Joe Panther wrapped their gloved hands around steaming cups of coffee. "How'd the ground look between here and the town?" Logan didn't bother to blew the hot liquid. He eyed Joe Panther over his cup.

"Seems to be fairly level. Snow ain't too deep. Going should be good."

Logan waited until Clarissa and all the men had refreshed themselves with hot coffee before he yelled, "Head 'em up . . . roll 'em out."

When Clarissa's group did reach the miner's camp in Dahlonega, the long, arduous journey didn't seem worth the trouble. The town was little more than dirty tents and ramshackle log huts clustered in a notch in the mountains, with a sprinkling of more of the same on the slopes.

An array of emotions assaulted Clarissa as her wagon entered the wide track of churned up mud and snow that served as Dahlonega's main street. She gazed at the two wooden structures of any size along the street. The first she passed was a saloon. The second, a general store.

By the time her wagons had pulled to a halt in front of the general store, she knew that, despite appearances, Dahlonega was bursting with wealth. Ragged, filthy miners crowded around the wagons. They yelled for clothes, flour, sugar, and tools—and gold was offered for what the miners demanded.

A group of men stormed Clarissa's wagon. She screamed, "Logan!"

194 *L. W. Rogers*

Just as quickly the teamsters took up positions on their own wagons to stop the rush.

The man who strode out of the general store was as anxious as the miners. He yelled, "Back off, men! Can't you see this here's a lady." He looked up at Clarissa and begged an apology. "Been a long time since we've seen a fair-skinned woman."

Logan rode his buckskin between the man and Clarissa's wagon. "You got a warehouse?"

The store owner looked up at Logan. "I do. And it'd be right smart if you sold everything in bulk to me rather than by piecemeal to the miners."

"Miss Hubbard is the owner of this outfit. You'll do business with her."

The man invited Clarissa to discuss the terms of the deal inside. Logan didn't think much of the man's chances of out-dealing Clarissa. He knew the smile she wore—one of pure innocence.

After exchanging a few more words with the store-keeper, Logan directed his teamsters around behind the store to the warehouse.

Logan smiled blandly as the store owner reached up and helped Clarissa down from the wagon. "Careful, Clarissa. The man's a guttersnipe."

Before going into the store, she turned to Logan. "Mind finding out if whoever owns that big saloon back there is interested in buying some decent liquor? Tell him I've got a whole wagon full."

"How much you want for it?"

The Twisted Trail 195

"Tell him I'll discuss terms with him myself, when he gets here."

Logan smiled at her. "What you mean is . . . you still don't trust me."

Her dark eyes warmed as they met his. "You know I do," she told him in a velvet-smooth voice. "Just not where money's concerned."

With that she walked into the general store. Logan still smiled as he turned back to his men. "Where's Tully?"

Joe Panther jerked a thumb toward the saloon.

"You and the men shoot anybody who tries to get close to the wagons." With that, Logan urged his gelding to the other side of the street.

He dismounted and entered the saloon. Tully Hayes stood at the bar, downing what was probably not his first whiskey. The old cowboy saw Logan come in and immediately got on the defensive.

Logan went past the bar without speaking to him. He found the owner of the saloon and told the man about Clarissa's wagon-load of liquor. The man went out as fast as he could without running.

This time Logan stopped at the bar. He looked at Hayes.

Hayes glared at him. "If'n you remember, I told you back in Fort Brooke that I didn't drink on the trail. And I didn't. We ain't on the trail no more . . . are we?"

The corners of Logan's eyes twitched as he suppressed a smile. "Do you hear me complaining?" He moved toward the door. Before opening it, he added, "I might

196   *L. W. Rogers*

be back in a bit. I could use a good drinking session myself."

He didn't expect the surprise that greeted him as he pushed through the door.

Sullivan stood outside less than twenty feet away.

Logan stopped. He didn't like the way Sullivan held his right hand, close to the gun holstered on his hip.

Logan kept his voice matter-of-fact. "So you got here."

Sullivan's voice was quiet, rigidly controlled. "Yeah. I got here. But my wagons didn't."

"Too bad. That's why we didn't use the pass you took. I figured some of those ledge trails would become impassable if a real blizzard hit."

"You know what this does to me?" Sullivan went on, the edge to his voice becoming apparent. "It means I lose every cent I put into those wagons. They'll be stuck there in the dead of winter, and come spring the Indians will steal me blind. You did this to me . . . you've ruined me."

"You ruined yourself." Logan's own voice was cold. "If you hadn't wasted everybody's time riding back and forth, trying to stop us, we'd *both* have gotten all our wagons here three, maybe four days ago. Before the snowstorm."

Sullivan wasn't listening. He said in the same tightly controlled, fury-driven voice, "I'm going to kill you, Logan."

No matter how crazy with anger Sullivan was, Logan didn't believe he was the type man for a face-to-face showdown.

The Twisted Trail 197

Logan did a quick survey of his surroundings. To his right was the saloon's outer wall. The hairs on the back of his neck prickled. He swiveled left. Novak stood there, standing in an opening between two brown-colored tents. His left arm cradled in a sling—a Colt in his right hand, pointed at Logan.

Logan twisted to face Novak, swerving to one side as he brought his own gun up from its holster. He fired at Novak as the gun cleared leather. Novak's shot roared a hair's-breath later.

A small black hole appeared in the middle of Novak's forehead. The force of the bullet knocked his hat off. Logan felt an enormous blow against the right side of his chest that nailed him against the saloon wall. His right arm went numb. His gun hand sank as he watched Novak topple forward.

Sagging against the wall, desperately fighting the agony in his chest and the darkness squeezing his brain, Logan tried to rally himself around for a shot at Sullivan. It seemed Sullivan's pistol moved in slow motion when he lifted it from its holster.

Logan found his own gun had become too heavy to lift with his right hand. Though he fumbled for it with his left hand, he couldn't seem to find it. Through blurred eyes he watched Sullivan leveling the pistol at him.

Joe Panther fired his rifle from the corner of the general store. The bullet smacked into Sullivan just below the breast bone and drove him backward. The revolver spilled from his hand. He clutched his chest, a look of mild surprise on his face. Then death changed his expression.

Logan watched Sullivan fall. His own legs gave way and he slid slowly down the wall until his knees touched the ground. He stayed that way, still holding the Colt in his right hand, squinting wearily at the dark shapes that moved toward him through the mists.

Grimacing against the awesome pain, he closed his eyes. The ghosts of his beloved wife and child beckoned to him. He thought of one Christmas Eve long, long ago . . .

Chapter Eighteen

Weeks later, Logan sat propped up on his bed in a log-walled room, playing solitaire on the blanket spread over his legs. He handled his right arm awkwardly, keeping it away from the bulge of bandages under his shirt.

For two days wind-whipped snow swept past the room's single window. He placed a jack on a queen. The door opened partway and Clarissa peeked in. Although his face was pale and much leaner than when they'd left Fort Brooke, she was glad to see the dullness gone from his eyes.

"Oh . . . you're awake."

"You know I am," he said in a bored voice. "It's past time for our poker game. You promised to keep me amused, remember?"

She held the salver with the coffeepot and two cups

in both hands while she used the toe of her shoe to nudge the door shut. She walked to the bed and sat the tray on a table next to it. "I was talking over a business deal with Big Mike, the man who owns the saloon."

"You're too damn money hungry. You could soothe your soul by spending more time with a sick man."

Clarissa scowled at him. "Dr. Smith says you're getting better every day. He expects you up and around in a few more days."

"A lot he knows," Logan grumbled. "The man is a horse doctor. I'm still weak as a baby."

"He isn't a horse doctor." Clarissa poured two cups of coffee and handed one to Logan. She eased down on the edge of the bed. "He's a dentist."

Logan harrumphed. "Horse doctor . . . dentist . . . one in the same."

"What difference does it make, Matt? He got the bullet out and saved your life."

Changing the subject, Logan said, "What's the good doctor predict about this blizzard?" He tossed the cards on the table.

She gathered the cards and smoothed them into a deck. "The old-timers around her say we're all going to be stuck in Dahlonega for at least another month. Horses won't be able to get in or out until the snow packs down hard enough to travel on. That's the reason for my business discussion with Big Mike this morning."

She dealt the cards with a fluid motion of her slender hands. "As long as we're going to be stuck here for a while, I thought I'd increase my profits."

The Twisted Trail 201

He gave her a bored looked, as if to say what's new. She ignored the look and continued to deal. "I've talked Big Mike into selling me the gambling concession."

Logan snorted and fumbled with the cards she'd dealt him. Clarissa continued, "I thought since this is a rough place for a woman to run gambling tables on her own, well, I thought you might be interested in going partners with me."

She looked at him the way she had the night when they'd camped out alone together under the pines. "We make a good team," she reminded him softly.

"You're sure you trust me with the money?"

"Shall we seal the partnership with a kiss?" she whispered the words as she touched his lips with hers.

The expression she wore reminded him that he wasn't a settling-down man. Not anymore.

It was almost as if she'd forgotten she'd dealt the cards. She gathered the cards he held, added them back to the deck, and reshuffled. Then dealt out two poker hands.

Logan noticed how she absentmindedly skimmed every other card from the bottom of the deck.

They smiled at each other.

"Clarissa," Logan leaned against the headboard, "what the devil are you after now?"

He caught her wrist as she fingerwalked her hand up his chest.

Her bewildered expression reminded him of what he needed to say. "Reckon I'll be moving on at the first signs of spring."

202   *L. W. Rogers*

She flushed and lowered her lashes. "I thought—"

"Don't look at me like that, Clarissa. You know what I'm talking about," he said. "We've shared some times together, and I'd be a fool to say I'm not attracted to you, but—"

Like the performer she was, he watched her mask whatever emotion she felt—disappointment, embarrassment, hurt. "I know." Her gaze slide away to look at the window.

The window rattled and shook in a sudden gust of wind, and snow flakes frosted the window pane. Logan's fingers closed firmly over hers.

"It might just be," he said, "an interesting way to spend a snowbound month."

They sat in thoughtful silence for a while. "This trip has changed me, Matt." Clarissa held the cards facedown on her lap.

His voice was gentle. "Maybe we've both laid some old ghosts to rest."

"You look tired," she said.

"I am." Logan smoothed a strand of dark hair from her cheek.

"It wouldn't last long between us, would it?" Her face showed she understood.

Logan sighed deeply. He nodded, but didn't speak. Instead, he kissed the knuckles on her hand.

Clarissa squeezed his fingers briefly, then pulled the covers high on his chest and left the room, quietly closing the door.